In London the blue-[illegible] capital had never kn[illegible] hold their breath. Those who saw it, and survived, knew what it meant and they would forever remember where they were standing, who they were with and what their thoughts had been when, for an instant, their world was lit up as if by a gigantic flashgun to give ten million people a picture that would never fade. But it went deeper than a photographic image. It went through to the marrow of the bones.

AFTERMATH

Roger Williams

A STAR BOOK

published by
the Paperback Division of
W. H. ALLEN & Co. Ltd

A Star Book
Published in 1982
by the Paperback Division of
W. H. Allen & Co. Ltd
A Howard and Wyndham Company
44 Hill Street, London W1X 8LB

Typeset by V & M Graphics Ltd, Aylesbury, Bucks
Printed in Great Britain by
Hunt Barnard Ltd, Aylesbury, Bucks

ISBN 0 352 31041 3

The extract from *Crow* by Ted Hughes is reproduced
by kind permission of Faber & Faber Ltd.

All characters are fictional. Any resemblance to persons living or dead is entirely coincidental.

'... the serpent emerged, earth-bowel brown,
From the hatched atom
With its alibi self twisted around itself'

Ted Hughes, *Crow*

1: THIRTEEN MINUTES

The dull piece of cord was about seven inches long, flattened and frayed at both ends and woven in a wishbone pattern. It was barely visible beneath the scum of muddy rainwater that had washed over the cracked red-tiled path the night before, but to Simon, squatting beside it, it was bright with life. He reached out a finger and poked at it to see if it would move. On the doorstep a few feet away Shirley had set down the shopping and was rummaging through her handbag for the key. She was certain she had put it in the bag, or as certain as she could be. It was caught in her cheque book.

'Come on, Simon.'

'It's a worm.'

'Is it?'

'A wiggerly worm. Can I eat it?'

'No. Come and carry some of my shopping.'

'Why?'

'Because the bags are heavy and I would like some help.' She emphasised each word, like a school teacher.

'No.' Simon stood up and drew a breath, an inverted sigh. 'I mean, why can't I eat it?'

Nearly six hours ago John had left for the office, taking Jenny to school on the way and picking up the car which they needed to go out to see friends that night – provided the babysitter turned up. But the car hadn't been ready and Shirley had had to collect it, picking up extra cash from the bank to meet the bill. The bank was always crowded on Fridays and Simon didn't understand queues. To crown it all the new clutch was stiff as starch and she had stalled half a dozen times in the impatient traffic round Shepherd's Bush on the way home.

Now she picked Simon up and carried him, heavy and awkward with reluctance, into the house. A struggling leg caught a packet of spaghetti sticking out of one of the carrier bags and, with no hand free to catch it, it toppled across the doormat. By the time Shirley had put the boy down the insidious goo of a carton of yoghurt was inching across the floor.

'Oh, bloody hell.' Her sudden swearing gave Simon a start and he began to cry. 'It's all right, love. It's not your fault. It was an accident. Come on, help me get a cloth to wipe it up.'

He sniffed. 'I want a pee.'

'All right, you have a pee. I'll get the cloth. Can you manage?'

He nodded moodily and headed for the stairs. When Shirley reached the tidy, modern kitchen the first thing she saw, staring up from the dresser like a stern reproach, was two letters which should have caught the midday post. One contained a cheque and the ultimate pink slip from the Gas Board. She wrung the cloth out furiously and wondered just how loudly she could scream. If the note were high enough she might reach a pitch nobody could hear, like a dog's whistle. That would be wonderful, to have her own silent scream with which she could go berserk without disturbing a soul. Simon called out from the bathroom.

'What is it?'

'I want some shampoo!'

'What for?'

There was a short silence which Shirley had come to know as the sound of foreboding.

'Teddy's having a bath.'

As she ran up the stairs the telephone in the hall started ringing. Not slowing down, she carried on into the bathroom where Simon looked up at her and smiled. He was a good-looking child.

'Shampoo,' he repeated and lifted Teddy, dripping, out of the loo.

After throwing the stinking bear into the bath and speechlessly bundling Simon out on to the landing and closing the door, she rushed back down the stairs to answer the phone. The front door was still open and all the yoghurt had slipped out.

'Shirley? It's Sue.'

Her neighbour lived only three doors away and Shirley wondered what made her call instead of dropping round. 'Hello,' she said slumping to the hall floor and catching sight of Simon picking distractedly at a corner of wallpaper. With an anguished tearing noise a strip a foot long came away.

'Have you heard?'

'Don't tell me,' Shirley said. 'They've just announced the end of the world.'

The siren had been whooping for more than two minutes and for half of that time Alan Reed had known what it meant. The Tannoy had broadcast the news like an abrupt sergeant major and, as with other messages that came crackling over the box in the corridor outside his office, he had no reason to believe that it wasn't true. Since the announcement he had made no movement except to raise his eyebrows and purse his lips. Madeleine had walked out on him two weeks ago in such a mire of mud-slinging that he didn't even wonder where she might be. There was no other family. Now he looked at his watch, the powder-blue cuff slipping evenly back on his wrist to reveal the square black face. When he pressed the button at its side it reported 13.51. He would miss the policy meeting. Dammit, that was a real regret.

The evidence against the Sales Director had been growing for weeks, but now office gossip had been substantiated by contacts Alan had beyond the politics of the building and the case against him was complete. The fact that he did not care for Jeffrey Bishop personally had, he liked to think, never come into it, but that hadn't stopped a glow like a draught of Drambuie coming over him each time another nail was banged into the man's coffin. He bent forward, pulled out a desk drawer and removed a file he had innocently marked 'Greengrass'. Opening it up on the desk in front of him he scanned the first page of the final indictment. For some time he had been preparing the way, letting the odd remark drop in the right channels so that the board would hear stories from every direction. But it would take more than rumour to sway them. They were impressed with bullshitters like Bishop, as though they thought that if now and then they could be fooled, then he must be a good salesman. They never stopped to think that others, hours later, may feel fooled too. Quite simply, he was bad for business.

'Greengrass' contained the last straw, the piece of evidence Alan would pull out after Bishop had scoffed at him and indignantly denied the other accusations. It had taken a while to piece together the statements and written scraps which were now all photocopied ten times, one set for each director. It was all so pathetic – a £200 backhander to the pensions department boss in a machine tooling company. But the pettiness of the deal, the insignificant amount of money, would show the thoroughness of the man's corruption. Caught with his trousers down, Bishop would undoubtedly say that that was the way business was today ('It's tough in the field. You desk jockeys don't realise what it's like out there.'). At which point Alan would take his cue, saying with characteristic restraint which would convey abundant reason that if that was the way the company wished to conduct its business then that was their affair, but he wanted no part in it. And he would offer his resignation, remembering as he did so to scoop the 'Greengrass' papers up off the boardroom table. Even if the directors still believed in Bishop and his methods, they would not be careless enough to let Alan go.

Now Bishop would never know what so many people thought of him, how transparent he really was and what trouble he had been. It was a shame but, worse than that, Alan realised, the news meant the whole matter might be reduced to complete unimportance. Nobody else in the company had known what he had planned, what a coup he had been about to pull off, and he longed to tell someone, even if it were the last thing he did. He decided on Beat. A wise woman, quick to laugh, she had never liked Bishop and they had often swapped stories about 'that man' over lunch. She was a great woman, he thought, as he tucked the file under his arm and headed for the door. If anyone would be appreciative or impressed by his efforts, Beat would – if she was still in her office.

He walked quickly down the corridor, the clonk of a typewriter growing louder as he progressed. When he reached Southern Area Accounts he put his head round the door and saw Miss Nielson at her desk.

'Hello,' he said.

She looked up briefly and nodded. Nearing fifty, she was

one of the longest-serving members of Pennines Assurance staff and her plain, solid looks conveyed the plod of her life spent in the company's service.

'Everything all right?'

'I'm just finishing some letters for Mr Mead,' she said, not breaking the rhythm of her fingers.

He wasn't sure what to say or suggest. 'I'm, er, on my way to get the key to the basement. Sounds a bit feeble, I know, but it might be worth a go.'

She nodded and Alan, thinking there was nothing else he could do, walked away. Ignoring the old lift, he took the stairs two at a time, thinking of Beat and the minutes he would spend with her. Perhaps they would kiss. Perhaps more. They had always got on well and although they often had lunch together if there wasn't much else happening, this was the first time he had thought of her in anything other than business terms. He remembered her shape, generous in a matronly sort of way, and for a moment he thought he caught a whiff of the rosewater with which she could distract a whole post-luncheon party coming back in the lift.

He was almost running by the time he reached the second floor and the corridor that took him to the teak-veneered door labelled 'Beatrix Simmons, Business Manager'. Alan stood just inside the room that wailed with the hollow sound of the sirens. She had gone. He had been cheated again and he swore. The expletive, however, was answered by a rustling behind the desk and Alan's first thought as he ran forward was that she must have fainted. He was met by the sight of a white fleshy arse. It wasn't Beat's. Somebody with similar ideas had reached her first. Jeffrey Bishop. Pressing himself up on two hands that straddled Beat's shoulders, he turned his balding head to look at Alan and give him a grin that tried to be knowing but which Alan thought merely stupid. He glowered at Beat and for a second he thought he saw a touch of guilt move through her brown eyes. Then they closed, the pupils turning upwards as if slipping into the unconsciousness of a *petit mal* and Jeffrey resumed the pumping rhythms that would end in death.

All feeling left Alan. He placed the 'Greengrass' file deliberately in the wastepaper basket and walked quietly away. At the door he said: 'I'm going to get the keys to the basement. It could be worth a try.' There was no reason for either of them to reply.

In Tothill Street, outside the Pennines Assurance company, a woman in a red suit, heavy-rimmed round glasses and swept-back hair sat at the wheel of a white Ford Fiesta and gazed at the traffic. It hadn't moved in several minutes and the stab she made on her horn was merely a sign of her impatience. She wound down the window and leaned out to see if she could discover the immediate cause of the blockage.

'No use hooting,' the driver of the Post Office van alongside her said. He had switched off his engine and was rolling a cigarette.

'I've got to get home. My basement flat's in the middle of the flood risk area.'

'Take the tube. You should have four hours before the river comes over the top – or so the posters say.'

She sat where she was, weighing up the cost of a flooded home against the abandonment of her car. 'How long have they been working on the flood barriers at Woolwich? Ten years?'

'More than that.'

Around them some people were leaving their vehicles, locking the doors behind them as they made their way down the street towards St James's underground station. Others, like the woman, continued to crane their necks, expecting to see a way out, or at least the reason for the sirens and the hold-up. A car mounted the pavement, its horn a continuous irate blast, scattering pedestrians like a child scaring pigeons in Trafalgar Square. Soon it was scraping a lampost which it could not get past and was wedged tight.

'Do you think we're high enough up here?'

'No idea.'

'You'd think the police would come and tell us what to do. Scotland Yard's only just over there. Perhaps there's something on the radio.'

She pressed a button in front of her. Immediately the newscaster's subdued voice told her what was happening and the white showed through the make-up on her cheeks. She struggled from the car, taking her handbag and not even bothering to close the door as she ran off down the street. The news from the radio reached the Post Office van and its driver muttered under his breath. He sat back and lit the cigarette.

In a small shabby office behind the Pennines building, John Hayley was listening to the engaged tone on his telephone. His toes were twitching in his thick-soled shoes and he stroked the side of his lean face at the edge of his trimmed goatee beard. Shirley must have got back from picking up the car by now and she was bound to have heard the sirens. Surely she would hang up soon, knowing he'd be trying to get through. He depressed the button on the top of the phone, dialled nine for an outside line, then tried his mother in Cambridge. She was engaged, too. He tried Shirley again, without success. Perhaps the lines were overloaded, perhaps the Post Office had already shut down all but Grade 1 lines. As much to check out the system as to call him up, he next tried the number of a colleague in another department, using a two-figure prefix that automatically put him through to the switchboard where he dialled the extension number. The ringing tone was unexpected.

'Philip Darby.'

'Philip, John Hayley. Is it a strike?'

'God knows. Everyone's making a run for it, though. Something's coming down. First casualties will be in the rush for the bunkers. What about your lot?'

'They're all out at lunch.'

'That should put their "exes" up this week ...'

'It's a bit sudden, isn't it? Not much warning.'

'Bloody odd. Anyway, we'd best hunker down as they say. Good luck.'

'Goodbye Philip.'

Drumming his fingers on the replaced receiver he said out loud, 'Bloody odd.' Then he tried his home number again but the line was still engaged. That would have to be it. Moving quickly now, he picked up his briefcase and emptied its contents into the top right-hand drawer of his desk, retrieving only a bunch of keys. From the top drawer he took out a bottle of soluble aspirin, from the top middle drawer a notepad, two biros and a pair of scissors. He put on his anorak and went into the next room where a secretary worked. From a tea tray beside a Busy Lizzie on a window-ledge he gathered up two half-full packets of biscuits, sugar, tea bags and an almost full carton of milk which he carefully placed inside the briefcase. A quick glance through the stationery cupboard produced only sellotape, and a ball of string. From the secretary's desk he took a bundle of keys which he jangled in his hand as he walked from the room.

Half-way down the corridor he stopped in front of a door, selected a key and opened it, leaving the bunch in the lock. Crossing the Grade 2 pile carpet to the Grade 2 wood desk, he took the central metal cannister of a table lighter out of its onyx base. This he put in his pocket as he hurried from the room and ran on down the corridor where there were no more doors, only a window at its end. When he reached it he put down his case and heaved up the casement to let in the full wail of the sirens, the hooting of the snarled traffic. Then he stepped out on to the metal fire escape and peered down into the basement well beside the alley. He was not surprised to see that his bicycle was no longer there.

Terence Latimer, Tel to his friends, eighteen and unemployed, gave the tube doors an extra shove to help them open. Skipping out on to the platform he ran along it ahead of the other passengers, his gym shoes taking him three at a time up the stairs. Before pulling lamely into St James's Park station the train had been stuck for five minutes in the tunnel, leaving him with nothing to do but grin at a pretty, fresh-faced girl with a red streak in her short fair hair who didn't want to know. His speedy exit was to escape the claustrophobia. It was only when he was half-way up the steps that he realised that the buzzing he had been hearing was not made by the train. Out in the day, above and in front of him, it was growing into an urgent whine and he looked up. There was an escalating crush of people, a rush-hour pack, and Tel remembered that this was Westminster, the paper capital of office workers and bureaucrats. It was Friday, of course, and everyone would be leaving early for the weekend.

At the top of the steps he had a different view. The subdued crowd, swelling quietly like an inflated lung, was being prevented from filtering through the barrier. Somebody in the ticket office was on the phone, his eyes occasionally darting up to check the crowd; outside it a group of half a dozen London Transport employees were in a huddle. When the man in the office came off the phone he leaned out of the door and spoke to his colleagues. One of them pushed his way to where Tel stood by the barrier and, turning to the crowd, said, 'All right, keep it orderly. Through the barrier only. One at a time.'

'What's going on?' Tel asked.

The collector, shuffling people through, barely looked up. 'Nuclear attack or something. In about ten minutes.'

Tel's eyebrows shot up. Behind him a trail of people was trooping down on to the platform where the train's motor had died and he remembered how oppressive the tunnel had been.

'I've got a date,' he said.

'Where's your ticket?'

Tel pushed twenty pence into the man's hand. 'From Westminster,' he lied.

The collector tutted in disbelief but he let him go. There was fifty pounds in Tel's pocket and he put his hand over it to keep it safe as he forced his way towards the exit in Petty France. The money was for his older brother, Bob, who had telephoned home from Horseferry Road Magistrates Court an hour earlier after unsuccessfully defending himself on a charge of speeding along the Embankment. He'd asked Tel to borrow the money off their Dad and bring it to the Two Chairmen where he would be rewarded with a drink and an hour or so of Bob's company.

As Tel progressed across the short distance to the street, the going was increasingly difficult and he shoved people firmly with his elbows. Conversation around him didn't go much beyond a banter which was greeted with exaggerated laughter: 'Don't suppose they're selling too many cheap days.'

'What's the hold-up, somebody trying to pay by cheque?' 'London Transport regrets . . .' Then from somewhere near the barrier there came a choked, sharp scream and the pack moved in that direction by about a foot. Without comment, people craned their necks, seeking a glimpse of some event between heads that bobbed like chickens'. Tel, taller than most at just over six feet, saw the girl from the train standing just inside the barrier, staring at a spot a few yards ahead. He was tempted to yell at her, to tell her to come with him and get out of the place. But he didn't. Instead he moved on. It was becoming hard enough to hold his ground, let alone progress against the tide. People were saying, 'Excuse me', 'Sorry', 'Ooops, was that you?', but the social graces were lessening, replaced by grunts as the seconds ticked by and limbs strained for space.

Then up ahead, from out in the sunshine, a police megaphone boomed. It told the people that if they had offices or somewhere else to go, then they should go there, not to the underground which would soon be full. Its deep, measured tones promised safety but not everyone was convinced and though some on the edges of the crowd out on the street turned around, most continued their shove towards the shelter of the station. When Tel finally broke clear of the crush he found he was standing in the middle of the road. Cars were jammed up all round, some abandoned, some with their drivers standing by, some still in their seats listening to their radios. To his right, at the corner of Tothill Street and Broadway, policemen were leaving the back of New Scotland Yard two-by-two, some striding out, others taking more tentative steps knowing they had to tell people to get inside buildings where they themselves should be. Some tried to make their way out on bikes, moving out past the white Rovers that sat gleaming and trapped by the kerb.

At the top of Queen Anne's Gate where it bore round to the right, a black-painted dormer window in the roof of a stern Baroque building opened and a man in shirtsleeves climbed out onto the ledge. If this thing doesn't happen, Tel thought, some people are going to look a bit silly. Turning the corner he saw the Two Chairmen, a small, dark, old pub ahead of him and he broke into a run. As he approached the sign of the sedan chair he caught the rising strains of 'We'll Meet Again', sung with great heart. It crescendoed to 'don't know whe-en' and the door was flung open and a chubby man in a crumpled jacket stepped carelessly out.

'Bob?'

'Tel, you made it.' His brother held out a welcoming hand. 'Got the monkey? Quick.' He grabbed at the offered notes. 'Back in a sec.'

He disappeared into the pub, leaving Tel alone on the pavement. The streets were clearing now. Nearly nine years his junior, Tel couldn't be anything but the family's youngest and when Bob said 'Jump', Tel still jumped. That was why he was there now with the fifty pounds. That and because he had nothing better to do. Since Bob moved out a few years back, they sparodically met up for beers and it was always good to see him. When he re-emerged he had a bottle of Scotch in each hand, one of which he handed over to Tel.

'Picnic in the park, I thought.'

'Yeah, why not. It's a nice day for it. Anyway,' he nodded towards the pub, 'I hate crowds.'

'Me too, they're getting harder and harder to stand out in.'

'Any rate, there's not much point in going with a whimper.' Tel seemed to be justifying the idea to himself more than making the point to Bob. He would go anywhere Bob went now and that would be that.

'That's right.' Bob swamped his throat with a great glug of Scotch. 'And with this lot inside us we'll go up a treat.' They passed under the arch into Cockpit Steps where a respectable looking man was pulling frantically at the chain of a bicycle locked to the railings.

'Watch out, it's the law!' The man looked round wide-eyed and Bob said, 'Ho ho,' then to Tel: 'How's Mum?'

'Not so good. The doctor said she should rest her leg for a week but I doubt she will.'

'She needs a holiday, that's what she needs.'

'That would be nice.'

'I've been thinking about that. I'll be off the uppers next week. There's some good deals coming up. Oh shit . . .' He stopped and his thick fist punched the air.

'What is it?'

'I left my briefcase in the pub. I don't want anybody finding it with what it's got in it. Keep going, I'll catch you up. Get the hamper ready, spread the rug, I won't be a jiff.'

Reluctantly Tel watched him go before starting out between the bumpers of the abandoned cars in Birdcage Walk, heading for the park.

At the pub the singing had stopped and when Bob reached the door he could hear nothing but the mumbling of a radio inside. The door was locked. He called for someone to come and open up but there was no reply and he turned down Lewisham Street, the alley beside the pub, to look for other doors. There were none. The sirens stopped for a second, taking a breath before they screamed again, and Bob looked at his watch. There was no more time. He ran quickly down the alley searching for clues: an open door, a beckoning finger, a friendly face that might pop out and say: 'Come inside!' But there was no one. Then he saw the manhole in the middle of the alley, its cover slightly askew. Taking a stern swig from his bottle he shifted the heavy disk to one side and peered into the reeking drain. Then he muttered: 'All right, Satan, here I come.' And he jumped in.

The old man not so much climbed as fell down the vertical, wood planked side of the hole in the road, landing with a damp thud on the yellow earth, his over-large grey wool coat spreading out over him. A sunken, unshaven face peered tortoise-like out of one end, its watery eyes fixed on the hole's only occupant.

'Think you're clever, do you, John? Think you can dig a hideout like this and not let anybody in? I know what you bastards do, looking after yourselves. Bunkers for the boys, that's it, isn't it? It's the same as last time – boudoirs for the generals, stinking bogs for the ranks. All in the same boat except you lot have got cabins. Well it's not happening again. Do you hear me? It's not going to happen again.'

Jack Parsons heard him all right, but he hadn't looked up after the first glance at the new arrival, and he carried on putting the finishing touches to a gas-pipe leak. When the news had come through his mate had run off but Jack had stayed to finish the job. If there were going to be fireworks, there was no point in giving them any help. He himself had no plans. His own place, in Acton, was too far to make for, and in any case a fourth-floor bedsit was no place to be even if he was going to live forever – or especially if he was going to live forever. In the end he had decided he would stay where he was, keep his head down in here and hope for the best. But now the drunk had dropped in, bringing with him the smell of urine and butt-ends and meths, an all-round aroma that reminded Jack too much of the nick. He'd have to take his chances outside.

'Where is it, then?' the drunk demanded, trying to get to his feet.

'Where's what?' Jack grunted.

'The wash room. The toy-let.'

Jack picked up his bag and started up the wooden ladder which was propped against the side of the hole. Without looking round he said: 'Why don't you piss in your boots, grandad, like you've always done.' He didn't bother to dodge the clod of earth that thumped against his thigh. Then he was over the top and out into the street. It was eerily quiet. From a long way away came the sound of klaxons, sirens and car horns, an audible sense of the city like the glow of a port from way out to sea. As he walked up the street, instinctively making in the direction away from the main road, he had an odd feeling, as if the law was running round in screaming circles, chasing itself.

The three-storey houses that lined both sides of the street were larger than most in the area. Smatterings of bell pushes around the front doors showed that most were divided up into flats, perhaps just single rooms, and the building rubbish in several gardens was evidence of the continual evolution inside the Victorian shells. But it wasn't until Jack had gone past half a dozen of them that he realised he had noticed something important. The houses on his side of the road had small grilles in the risers of the front door steps. That meant that there had to be cellars underneath. Number 52 was unusual not just because there was a single bell beside the door but also, Jack noticed with a grin, by a second-floor window was a burglar alarm. Though the curtains were all drawn, the new, unpainted front door was ajar. He pushed back the iron gate and walked up the path, spilling mud from his boots over the dull red tiles. It didn't occur to him to knock and, after stepping over a puddle of white liquid spilled on the threshold, he stood for a moment on the beige carpet just inside the door.

The entrance to the cellar would, he presumed, be under the stairs, and that was where the child's whine was coming from. Jack walked down the hall to the open cellar door, wondering if the child were on his own. But before he had a chance to find out he was stopped by the sound of footsteps clonking up the bare wood stairs from the dimly-lit room below. There was Shirley, her fair hair in glistening streaks and her small eyes bright with fright. An empty bucket fell from her hand, tumbling down the stairs, and her shriek threatened to bring neighbours from four blocks away. Jack didn't move, keeping her in the shadow of his bulk.

'You on your own?' he asked, and his eyes roamed over her body.

'Who are you?' The lump that had caught in her throat made her whisper.

'Jack Parsons.'

She took a deep breath to find her voice again, which, when it came, had the same school-teachery sound it had when she spoke to Simon. 'Well, Mr Parsons, this is my house and you are trespassing.'

'Who's down there?' he wanted to know.

'My son. He's three.' She said it as if the innocence that Simon's age conveyed was also a sign of her own incorruptibility, then she added: 'But my daughter and husband will be home any minute . . .'

'What are you doing down there?'

She pushed past him. It seemed silly to explain, to say that she was trying to act sensibly by getting herself and her son down into the cellar with whatever provisions she could find. So she just said: 'What do you think?'

'Everything you've got, lady. You'll need it all. Not just the tinned food. Take your flour and rice and dried foods as well.'

'Look . . .' she began, but he had overtaken her and was in the kitchen going through the cupboards.

'Coffee, tea bags, let's get them shifted. Your booze and medicine cabinet as well. How about water?'

'There's an old laundry tub in the cellar. It's nearly full.'

'All right, fetch the bucket up and I'll do the rest.'

Although Shirley returned to the cellar, she really did not know what to do. Whatever she said to the intruder, it was clear he was not going to go away. It was sacrilege that he should come into their lives at a time like this, yet his assertiveness and implacability had been oddly reassuring, like somebody stepping into a dream to tell them it wasn't real. In the corner of the musty cellar Simon looked up at her.

'Who's that?'

'A man.'

'What man?'

'Just a man.' She picked up the bucket and he ran towards her, holding tight to her skirt. 'Come on, Simon, I must go and fetch some water.'

'No,' he shouted. 'Stay here.'

'Simon, I must.'

'Nooooo.'

The light from the top of the stairs was suddenly blocked. 'You stay down there, lady, with the kid.' It was a command. 'Get in a corner. I'm going to chuck things about.'

There was no time for a reply before six drawers, complete with their contents, came crashing down the steps. Silently, obediently, Shirley and Simon crouched in a corner as bread, cake and biscuit tins bounced down around them.

'Got any candles, lady?'

'In the cupboard under the sink.'

There was the sound of shelves being cleared by the armful, then another explosion as more stores were hurled down the stairs. As crash followed crash, Simon became increasingly perturbed. With one hand Shirley held him firmly, with the other she stroked his hair, and she started to sing. Her fingers were just inches from his Adam's apple and if the pain became too much she prepared herself to press it deeply, lovingly in.

2: TWO CITIES

At the new Skean Dhu hotel at Altens in the south of Aberdeen, councillor Alisdair Johnson was in the lounge bar with two men who were in oil. It was part business, part pleasure, for though he played golf with one of them now and then, the councillor tried to meet up with them about once a month to catch up on their companies' gossip and problems. As the news crackled on the paging loudspeakers, everyone strained to listen to make sure they had heard right. Heads twisted backwards and forwards looking for the reactions of others in the bar. Then Johnson was on his feet, sprinting to the phone, leading the rush from the bar. He couldn't believe it. It wasn't meant to happen this way; it wasn't meant to happen this way at all. First he tried the city council offices at Town House. The number was engaged. Then he tried the regional offices. They were engaged, too. So was the Lord Provost, the chief executive – both office and home numbers – and the police station. He had carefully remembered the direct line to the general at the army's Highland headquarters in Perth but when he began to dial it the numbers fled from his mind. Directory enquiries was engaged. In desperation he finally dialled 999.

'Emergency, which service do you require?'

'Police.'

The line went dead for a moment before a quiet, reasonable voice came on the line.

'Police emergency service. Can I help you?'

'This is councillor Johnson, can you put me through to the chief constable?'

'I'm sorry, sir, this is the emergency service only.'

'Can you get him to call me?'

'I'm sorry, sir, this is the emergency service only.' He hung up.

If he were to reach the Town House in Union Street in the time the radio said was left, he could not wait to try to get through to anyone else. Pushing his way through a forest of tall men and shining suitcases, a newly arrived oil crew, he ran out through the vivid yellow foyer and into the car park where the rush to escape, to get home or out of town had turned the place into a dodgem arena. Digging both his hands into his trouser pockets to save time looking in each one for his keys, he grabbed at the bunch, unlocked the car door and climbed in. Before he could get away there was a heavy thumping on the roof and he opened the passenger door to let his lunch-time companion in.

'You brought me here, you might at least take me home.'

'I'll drop you off up the road.' He turned north into Wellington Street towards Victoria Bridge that would take him over the Dee and up Market Street to the Town House.

'What did you find out?'

'Nothing.'

'What are you supposed to do now?'

'A million things. We're meant to have a week's warning about this sort of thing, if not two. It's crazy, look at all this traffic coming out of town. Somebody should be stopping them. The emergency services will never get through. All the roads should be sealed off round the town and people should stay put as it said in the broadcast. There's the electricity and gas and oil to think about, and there are things to commandeer . . .'

His companion laughed. 'Is my company included in your commandeering plans?'

'Take it seriously, man. It's happening. It's on the radio.'

'But not Aberdeen. The rigs are way out to sea and the oil doesn't come ashore here. There are dozens of strategic targets all over the world before they get round to us.'

'Any part of the oil business is strategic, just as any city is . . .'

But he couldn't finish what he was saying. A distant growl had grown into a shrieking roar, the nerve-wracking noise of more than a million pounds' worth of aggression as an American F-16 flew directly over their heads, hurtling towards Aberdeen Bay on a path so low that eardrums threatened to burst. And though they couldn't see them, they could hear others, further out to sea, which must have been practically surfing by the booming sounds that smacked against the land. Most of the traffic had come to a stop by the sight of it, but the councillor kept going

'They don't waste time,' his companion said. 'Where are they from?'

'Edzell, I suppose.'

'I didn't know it was an air base.'

'They get visitors from time to time. Can I drop you off here?'

His companion got out. The councillor was sweating now. The aircraft had unnerved him, their highly-strung screaming still whistling in his ears, and he began hooting his horn as he sped along. His hoots were answered by others from the cars going in the other direction. At the top of Wellington Road he ignored the one-way system that diverted traffic down on to the Esplanade and the fish market that was always caught up with lorries and instead continued along Menzies Road which was now the preserve of buses. Almost immediately a police motorcyclist overtook him and forced him to stop.

'This street is for buses only,' he said leaning over the car.

Johnson was nearly out of his skin with agitation. 'Look, I'm Councillor Alisdair Johnson and I need to get to the Town House. I'm the City's Emergency Planning Officer.'

The policeman frowned. 'What does that mean?'

'It means that I am in charge of making the arrangements to defend Aberdeen in the event of a nuclear attack.'

'Oh, good. You'd better be on your way, then.'

At the end of the road, however, as he turned to go over the bridge, the traffic coming out of the city was stuck fast, bottled up by vehicles from the Esplanade. In a panic, he leapt from the car and ran over the bridge. To his right was the harbour, spread out, where small figures ran to and from the ships, the supply boats and the ferries that went to the Shetlands and the Orkneys. Skirting the cars and avoiding the pedestrians who were joining the exodus from the city, he was nearing the far side of the bridge when he heard a shout. A man was pointing into the air. He stopped for a moment to look up, too. At first he could see nothing. Then the sun caught a glint of metal, just a speck high above them, which disappeared almost as soon as he saw it. Another shout and he looked to the east, following the direction of another pointed finger. He could see nothing there. He looked back to the first speck. There was something there now, the light continuing to reflect on its side, a thin vapour trail. There was no doubt about it. Whatever it was, it was going to pierce the shining mail of the granite city.

A few miles west of Bishop Auckland, Dr Iain MacGilvray, a consultant physician at Durham's Dryburn Hospital, was catching up on some fishing. He had crumbled pieces of pie in his fingers which were a little stiff from arthritis – 'the pains', as some of his patients called it – and tossed them into the water to attract the fish. Not for the first time in the past few months he began to wonder what he might be doing this time next year. He had been south for most of his life and he was quite happy here but with the approach of retirement he increasingly felt a desire to settle in Inverness again. Perhaps he would try it out with a long holiday, and he wondered which relations he could impose himself on.

At first the light flash was little more than a blink of the sun, a trick of the light among the conspiracy of trees that came down the steep banks in front and behind him. A second later the flash was unmistakable, a blinding light that whipped across the treetops with a force, temporarily upsetting his sense of colour, turning the spring leaves to a strange yellow for an instant and shimmering the muddy coloured water with a sparkling white as if it were charged with electricity. To his right two objects splashed into the water. A minute later came the explosion, an almighty boom which shook through his boots and echoed again and again through the hills and the valleys around him. As the sound rumbled away so too did the slight humming which had been troubling his ears for the past ten minutes.

Oh, Christ, he thought, another Flixborough; but as he gathered up his tackle, almost snapping the rod as he dismantled it, he searched his memory in vain for any industry which might have caused it. The two objects that had fallen into the river floated past and he could see they were two birds, charred as charcoal, with not one feather left to show what they had been.

3: GLASS, WIND AND FIRE

In London the blue-white flash brought with it a silence the capital had never known before. Even buildings seemed to hold their breath. Those who saw it, and survived, knew what it meant and they would forever remember where they were standing, who they were with and what their thoughts had been when, for an instant, their world was lit up as if by a gigantic flashgun to give ten million people a picture that would never fade. But it went deeper than a photographic image. It went through to the marrow of the bones.

In Queen Anne's Gate the full melting force of the flash hit the shirtsleeved man who had been standing on the window-ledge seven storeys up. With who knows what fears of death or fatal, lingering injury he had jumped a split second beforehand. Now his shadow was scorched on the stone face of the building fifty feet from the ground and the impression of his tie, whipping upwards as he fell, was also there, rising like a hangman's noose.

Round the corner, beneath the budding branches of the plane trees, Tel had been walking slowly over the grass towards the spanner shape of St James's lake. The park was mainly cleared of the sun-seeking lunchtime crowd who had scurried back to the shelter of their offices just as the radios and police megaphones had asked. A few groups of seeming fatalists remained, either not believing it or wanting to be wiped out in the initial blast. One or two stragglers wandered undecidedly, torn between official instruction and a nagging nihilism. Tel had not gone far into the park when curiosity took him up a small incline topped with a bushy border that was concealing something he could not quite see. Walking on the earth between the shrubs and trees he came to a bare wood picket fence through which he saw a recessed compound with concrete walls five feet high around the sides. To the left was a mound of collected litter, to the right piles of earth and sand and, beyond them, a tractor and two trailers.

Tel was never sure exactly what happened. One minute he

was wondering if he should climb down into the hollow or if he should stay in sight of the passageway so Bob could see him. The next, he was imbedded in the pile of earth fifteen feet away, his closed eyes bright with the image of a yellowing sun. He had heard no explosion.

The shock wave that followed twenty seconds after the flash did, however, make a noise, a roar that for most people devastated the silence and shook them from the stunning implications of the flash. Between St James's and the source of the disaster there were acres of solid buildings and the people jostling round the station had been largely protected from the burning light. But when the explosion came they were completely vulnerable. Outside the north entrance in Petty France more than a thousand windows in the fourteen-storey Home Office building erupted, tearing to shreds those left behind in offices and cascading down into the street, smashing on the road and pavements and leaving no one alive. Some shards flew inside the station's booking hall where they stabbed like slashing ice-picks and in the shower of blood there were shouts and screams. 960 sheets of glass, each measuring about ten feet by five, caved in at the back of New Scotland Yard, piercing those outside the eastern entrance to the booking hall, in Broadway.

In Tothill Street the Post Office van shook with the eruption and the driver, staring blankly at his shattered windscreen, listened to the monstrous hailstorm on his roof. A slight shiver went through him and his body felt clammy. He looked down at it. Though he had been protected from the shower above, his open door had let in glass that bounced up from the pavement. His right side, from his chest down, was in bloody tatters. There was no immediate pain but he knew he did not have long to live and he took the cigarette from where it was stuck to the gory crippled fingers of his right hand. He puffed at it but it had gone out.

By far the worst carnage caused by glass was on the other side of New Scotland Yard in Victoria Street. On both sides of the road for more than half a mile thousands of gleaming panes from modern office blocks hit the ground in a deafening timpany. A bus keeled over, the jam of cars buckled in and several hundred bodies pumped their life blood into the street beneath the sparkling blanket of broken glass. Among them were several policemen who had been urging people to get indoors, though with the glass blowing inwards, too, few could have survived in the rooms behind the flat facades.

At the river end of the street, on the north and east faces of Big Ben, the clock's giant hands measuring nine and fourteen feet had warped and bent, leaving time standing as a shadow at one minute past two. The light above it, which would have been turned on that night to show parliament was in session, had exploded but the building had already been evacuated. The dun-coloured elaborate spires that made the building so distinctive toppled over, the first layer of the parcel to be opened up. Five minutes later the scorched clock tower cracked, crumbled and fell.

Across the street the twin squat spires of Westminster Abbey shook and soon they, too, would be down. Inside, the dean, dressed in his working suit, stopped his prayers and, since the crypt was already overflowing with women and children, he begged the remaining congregation to hide beneath the pews. He could think of nowhere else for them to go. At the other end of Victoria Street, the Catholics had less warning. The scorched red camponile of Westminster Cathedral shook queasily and with a diabolical thunder of bells 283 feet of Victorian brickwork spilled down across the four-domed roof, hurling brick and mortar down on those who had sought safety there. The altar's columns bowed outwards as if an invisible Samson had pushed them, and mosaic chips flew around like gold coins spilled from the money-lenders' tables. Looking up, those left alive could see silhouetted before the ceiling's gaping holes the huge crucifix, still fastened to the nave arch, swinging slowly back and forth through the billowing dust, its shadow searching out the souls rising from below.

The epicentre of the blast was, as it happened, Sadler's Wells Theatre in Rosebery Avenue, EC1, a little more than two miles to the north east. There was no matinee that afternoon but the Royal Ballet was just beginning rehearsals for a new production of Giselle. The 200-kiloton device was equivalent to 200,000 tons of TNT and therefore a small weapon in the world's arsenal, which contained bombs many hundred times more powerful. Nevertheless, it was about fifteen times more potent than Little Boy, the atomic bomb that flattened Hiroshima.

From a crater fifty yards across and half as many deep, shock waves penetrated underground, cracking gas pipes and cables and, travelling down storm pipes and suppressed water systems, broke the banks of Regent's Canal in several places. Its water, which would soon be contaminated with deadly radiation, found its way into parts of the Central, Piccadilly, Victoria and Northern Lines. Two per cent of the city's population were crammed into the underground, and though some flood gates had closed they were little use, since they had been designed to stem a tidal wave coming from the river Thames. St James's Park, close to the surface and on the distant District Line, was safe from the many tons of water that were collecting in the deepest tunnels but in the darkness, with entrances blocked first with the dead and then with falling slabs of concrete, those who had sought refuge there might not have thought themselves particularly blessed.

Anyone within a mile of the epicentre who had survived the impact of the explosion, the collapsing buildings and the shattering glass had only thirty seconds to live. A second, blinding fireball lammed across this distance consuming everything in its sun-hot belly. As the fire raged at around 2000° Centigrade it needed air to fuel it and it sucked greedily, pulling in winds up to 200 miles an hour which brought with them fallen debris, trees, cars, people. At its nub the heat swirled upwards, taking with it material scraps, to join the greying mushroom cloud. Hundreds of feet up the air cooled, spread out and began to fall and sparks and torches of burning debris began their journey back to earth. On the ground the firestorm scorched the heart out of King's Cross, Islington, Shoreditch, Clerkenwell, Bloomsbury, and stuck flaming tongues out towards Soho and the golden square mile of the City. In the British Museum the plundered art treasures of more than two millennia were buried as the vast, monolithic edifice collapsed. In the National Gallery, canvasses worth countless millions were consumed in flames. The Barbican, so long in the building, swiftly became a pile of red rubble. Office giants toppled in the City and the vulnerable Nat West Tower fell beside the crushed dome of St Paul's. The Post Office Tower was down, and high rises that no amount of enlightened planning could eradicate disintegrated from the South Bank to Euston. On Hampstead Heath the eyes of those who had been looking towards the city had melted and the light flash had crippled the Crystal Palace Mast seven miles to the south. Buildings were damaged from Battersea to Stratford, from Brixton to Golders Green, from Notting Hill Gate to Deptford, and in the fires that would follow there was liable to be little left between the City and the mouth of the Thames.

Beneath the narrow alley of Lewisham Street, in a tunnel which had recently been re-faced with concrete, narrowing it to two feet wide by four feet high, John Hayley heard the booming explosion echo along a tunnel up ahead. He was on his hands and knees, his head pulled back to listen to any signs that the city's decaying sewage system could not withstand the blast. His question was soon met by the sound of falling bricks, a clang behind him and a distant thunder of collapsing roofs that lasted several minutes. The sound came from the east, to his left, though as it died away he thought he heard a muffled crash, this time from nearby, to the west. Then there was another, different sound, a voice behind him saying: 'Bloody hell.'

Although he could see nothing in the blackness, John tried to turn round to make out who was there. 'Hello?' His voice echoed damply.

'Yoohoo,' Bob called back.

'How many of you are there?'

'Just the one, squire. Got a table by the door?'

'What?'

'Never mind.'

'Come on, shift forward,' John instructed. 'We'll move down here to the main tunnel where we can stretch our legs. Did you shut the manhole cover?'

'It shut itself – on my head.' Bob took a swig from his bottle and limped forward on a hand and knees, one hand ensuring the continued safety of the bottle of scotch. 'Got a light?'

'Best to save it. Just keep coming. It slopes down a bit, but it's quite straight, no corners. Should be there in a couple of minutes.'

Dragging his briefcase, John crawled forward with cautious confidence, thinking they must be passing now beneath Central Hall and would soon be under Parliament Square where the lower of the three main sewage tunnels north of the Thames ran, east to west. He knew he was nearing it when a distant roar came to him as if through a megaphone a few feet away. He stopped abruptly and was immediately irritated by Bob's scraping movements and the younger man's heavy breathing. Then, in a rush of panic, John realised what the approaching sound might be. Anything that exploded in or near the river, even in the estuary half-way out to sea, would cause a stupendous tidal wave to race up-river, and he cursed himself for not thinking about it on the many occasions when he had mulled over his escape plans.

He braced himself against the wall and called out to Bob: 'Hang on!' But the roar whistled past the tunnel, west to east, without so much as a splash. It was a furious wind and it caused a vacuum in the smaller tunnel, taking their breaths away.

'Can't ... air ...' Bob gasped.

'Hang on.' John took his briefcase in both hands, reached forward to the tunnel's mouth and stuck it out to act like a fin, diverting the passing gale. It did little more than swirl around.

'Any better?' he called.

Bob's heavy hand fell on his ankle. 'Not much.'

John wondered what else to do. Then he spread his body flat, face down, and braced himself. 'Climb on top of me.'

Not giving up his bottle, Bob struggled, coughing, along John's back until their heads were level. There he could breathe better and he gulped down the rancid air as the wind buffeted his hair, reminding him of the cuffings he once received from his dad.

He felt a little better, less constricted around his chest, and he said to John lying beneath him: 'If the Met Commissioner could see us now he'd think that anarchy had broken out.'

Though not usually overtaken by humour, John saw the joke and found it unexpectedly funny. Beneath Bob's fourteen stone he nearly broke a rib trying to let out a laugh.

'It's all right,' said Bob. 'The wind's dropping. I'll move off.' And he shifted back down the length of John's body to take another swig. 'Pongs a bit in here, doesn't it?'

'At least we're alive.'

'Where does it go?'

'All along by the river. I'm hoping it's still open as far as Hammersmith.'

'I'll be off the other way. Does it stop by Malmesbury Road in Bow?'

John shook his head, a futile gesture in the dark. 'No use that way. That's where the cave-ins were and that's the way the wind was blowing. It means the bombs have dropped east of here. So even if you could get through, you'd be walking right into it. The fires could last for days. Then there's the radiation ...' His voice trailed off as he thought of the world outside.

'Well, if it ain't one damn thing, it's another. Is it time to see what's happening?'

'Give it a couple of minutes.'

They sat and waited. It was hard to collect any thoughts together and Bob wasn't so sure that it was great to be alive. It seemed as if the greatest part of his life had just evaporated. His flat in Bow, his family in West Ham. It was as impossible to imagine now as it had been when the sirens sounded. Why hadn't he believed them instead of fooling around, trying to get his case from the pub? This wasn't where he should be, he should be in the park with Tel, whatever was going on out there.

John, on the other hand, was glad to be alive and he had, he believed, every reason to be optimistic. The destruction definitely sounded as if it had been in the east and with any luck his family would be safe, but he needed desperately to know. He only hoped Shirley had been at home, where she would know to shelter from the fall-out in the cellar. They had talked about the possibility of a nuclear attack more than once before.

Forty yards west of John and Bob was another tunnel, similar in size and function except that the skimping of successive governments had left it unstrengthened. The old brickwork had not been cemented over and it caved in, bringing down the earth it had supported for more than a hundred years and this tumbled from the end, forming a steep slope down into the sewer.

Above it was the basement of the Pennines Assurance Building, a large windowless room dominated by a boiler which heated the six floors above. Otherwise there were some of the house manager's stores, cleaning equipment, two filing cabinets and boxes of old records and correspondence which hadn't quite been thrown away. The unplastered walls were painted white, two bare bulbs glowed near the ceiling and there was a smell of cleaning fluid. Less than a minute before the first flash the door at the top of the wooden stairs had opened and Jeffrey Bishop was urging Beat Simmons in. His hand on her upper arm forced her quickly down the steps as he looked about the room to see who else was there.

'Reed?' His blunt call was like a summons.

From behind the boiler the younger director appeared with a box in his hands and his lean face showed no sign of being pleased to see them. The couple reached the bottom of the stairs just as the lights went out, exploding with a single pop. The image of each other was trapped in the screaming, silent darkness that followed and in which each hardly dared to breathe. Then Beat said, almost whimsically, 'Is this goodbye?' and was answered almost immediately with the first crashes of the explosion. The two men, already unnerved by the pistol crack of the bulbs, immediately hit the floor but Beat stayed where she was, standing against the wall and gripping tightly to her handbag. Above them, beyond the door at the top of the steps, their offices, their firm, their livelihoods, were being savagely destroyed.

Bishop, his hands over his balding head, saw his black button-backed chair being disembowelled by hunks of plaster and concrete and in the small lecture room he saw his new video equipment smashed to smithereens. Boiling with a livid hatred for the foreign power, the stupid, blinkered, bloody-minded communists who had caused his world to crack apart so suddenly, he muttered: 'Bastards.'

As sounds of desecration continued, some nearby, some far away, his mind travelled away from the confines of his work on which he had ridden, blossomed, thrived for so many years, and he thought of his family in the detached modern house in Enfield. The eldest girl, who worked in the City, was getting married in a month and there was to be a marquee in the garden. He saw her face, not pretty but soulful, a little lost, and he longed now, this minute, to give her that day with its ridiculous extravagance. The boy, who last year had found a flat in town, was, mercifully with any luck, on holiday in France. The younger girl was still at school and had stayed at home today complaining of a stomach ache. The recollection also brought to mind his wife and he thought immediately of his infidelities. There he was, brought to account before the flattering ranks of women he had known, all smiling now and remembering the best times. Among them, last and somewhat least, was Beat and he was brought back from his daydreams to realise the sounds were dying and she was standing by his side.

'Beat?' He put concern into his voice. 'Are you all right?'

'Yes, Jeffrey,' she said coolly and he suddenly felt rather foolish lying on the floor.

He stood up. 'Christ that was one hell of a bang.' As soon as he had said it he saw the double meaning and before Beat might have a chance to say otherwise he hurried on: 'What's happening? There was nothing in this morning's papers.'

'I don't know.' She was cautious now, firmer than the limp and pliable mind and body she had become after they had heard the announcement up in her office. It never occurred to Jeffrey whether he liked her or not. Certainly, despite their similar ranking in the company, he had not given her much thought. She was fairly sensible, he supposed, and wasn't bad company in a pub, but of all the board members he listened to her opinion least. As for any other thoughts about her, well, she was plump and nearly his age: what more was there to say? Yet her ardour and almost total domination of him ten minutes ago had taken him somewhat by surprise until he had brought the unexpected pleasure to an abrupt and hopeless finish after the departure of Reed. The interruption had made him think that perhaps, despite the cliche, there might be a better way to go. It had been his turn then to be nervous and he had persuaded Beat to go with him to the basement. On the way down neither of them had spoken.

A few yards in front of them Alan's implacable features began to glow beside a lighted candle. 'Did you hear that?' he asked. Jeffrey was still thinking of a silly answer to a silly question when Alan said: 'It came from somewhere over here.'

He walked towards their right and bent down with the candle to examine the curling grey lino. There was a slight breeze on the back of his neck and the flame snuffed out. He stood to one side and lit it from a lighter once again.

'What is it?' Beat went over to him and in the shadowy light Jeffrey noticed her black skirt was caught up at the back. She hadn't put her tights back on, and her ankles, he thought, looked blotched and far from feminine.

'Something's collapsed under here.'

'It's getting warm,' she said. The others had noticed it, too. It had been cool when they arrived but now the temperature had risen several degrees and was starting to be uncomfortable. 'Do you think there's a fire?'

Alan let a derisory puff of air escape from his nose. 'Bound to be.'

'Christ, is that boiler working?' Jeffrey saw the implications.

'No. Everything's off. There don't seem to be any mains electrics down here either. Will someone hold this candle?'

Someone was clearly Beat, since she was standing next to him, but he didn't look at her as she took the candle from him. The cracked lino ripped back easily and it wasn't long before several square yards had been removed to reveal the dusty boards beneath.

'What's down there?' Beat asked.

'No idea, but the way things are going,' he nodded at the flickering candle, 'it won't be long before we run out of air. We need something to prise these boards up with. Quickly.'

'Can't we just go out the door we came in by?' she suggested.

'This is nuclear.' Alan sounded as if he was addressing muddle-minded geriatrics. 'Apart from the fact that half the building is probably piled up behind the door, when the shock waves stop you don't just walk out into it.'

'Anyway,' said Jeffrey, smiling, 'Reed likes digging deep.'

Alan looked at him sharply and his eyebrows unintentionally bobbed in deep suspicion.

Perhaps there was some fun left after all, Jeffrey thought, getting this son-of-a-bitch riled. He was feeling more relaxed now. Maybe the sex had helped. It was a joy to stand there and watch Alan growing taut as a piano wire, taking it out on the floorboards. The first board to come up, prised loose by a filing cabinet's metal rod, caused most difficulty but after that brute force tore away a dozen others. Beneath them was a hole two feet deep that smelled of dampness and decay. Taking off his Savile Row suit jacket, Alan dropped into it and immediately the floor shrank several inches, downwards and to the left. Dustpans from the cleaners' cupboard were what he wanted now and once again it was Beat who did his bidding. But as she handed the implements to Alan she said sweetly: 'Why don't you lend us a hand, Jeffrey?'

'It's a daft idea,' he said. 'At least there's four walls round us here and a roof over our heads.' But he stepped forwards to help anyway.

The hole wasn't big enough for two, so Beat and Jeffrey stood by its opening, dispersing piles of earth and rubble, and ensuring that the candles from the house manager's stores gave sufficient light. For his part, Alan worked like a man possessed, plunging the dustpans into the earth in the direction he had slid and scooping bricks and clumps of mortar up in his hands, until his knuckles bled and palms swelled with abrasions. The sweat of his labours, of fear as the earth beneath him slipped more than once around his feet, of determination that his efforts should be rewarded, ran from him in torrents. In some way he was also trying to escape from the betrayal of Beat Simmons and the deliberate effrontery of Jeffrey Bishop.

Back in the other tunnel, John sensed the wind was dropping and, goaded by Bob's unpleasant coughing, he decided it was time to take a look. He pushed his legs out of the end of the pipe and sat there listening. A small but continuing breeze meant he had to shield the flame from his match and it showed little of the large tunnel that disappeared dark and dank in front of him. He estimated it would be about twelve feet across and ten feet high and that the floor, which should be dry enough after more than a week without rain, would be about four feet below him. What he hadn't reckoned on was the smell of cess and filthy household water that swamped his guts. The match burned out and he took from his briefcase the ball of string and scissors. Then he emptied the contents of his pockets into his case, took off his anorak and began methodically cutting strips off the thick padded sleeves.

'What's going on, General?' Bob called.

'I'm just cutting up my anorak.'

'Well that's fine by me if it's all right with you.'

'When you get to the end here,' John went on, 'sit on the edge, tuck your trousers inside your socks and tear up some clothing to tie round your legs and ankles.'

'Good idea, General. Any special reason for it?'

'Yes. The rats.'

John had a fair idea of what would happen in a nuclear attack and he and Shirley both knew something of what to expect. When she had been pregnant with first Jenny, then Simon, there had been moments of worry about bringing a new life into such a world. Now, crouched in the cellar with the younger of the children, the anguish of the anticipation was almost as great as any physical suffering the explosion might bring. With her fingers pressed close to Simon's throat, with her daughter and husband elsewhere and a trespasser roaming about her home, she was petrified. In the absence of anyone to turn to she looked for spiritual solace. It was hard to know what to ask of God, to whom she had not spoken since her early teens. Not forgiveness, not love, nor, after such a long silence, did it seem right to beg for favours. So she simply repeated the Lord's Prayer over and over again.

It was instinct that had brought her hand close to Simon's throat, a terrible fear that she might have to see the child suffer. Only then, if he were in real agony, would she be forced to this last resort. Instead of the expected explosion, however, the first disturbance was the door at the top of the stairs into the cellar slamming shut and Jack crashing in on them. In a glance he took in the picture of the two of them huddled together, saw the intended gesture of her right hand and bellowed: 'Leave him alone!'

In the next second there was a curious feeling, of a light that wasn't there, of a presence that didn't exist, an aura that contained a deathly silence that might herald a divine miracle. The cellar's single bulb popped. For nearly a minute the only movement was from the small breaths of the boy. Then came a single sound, a roaring boom which shook the house around them, punishing their eardrums and flailing their nerves. Nothing else. Nothing to see, nothing to feel. Only the knowledge that a nuclear force was now unleashed; a moment the world had been waiting for since the arms race began. The vibrations continued and Shirley listened, wondering if there would be more, wondering if and when her home would fall down.

'Is that thunder? Why's it dark?'

'No, it's not thunder. Something's gone off bang.'

'Like a balloon?'

'Bigger than a balloon.'

As the earth-shaking vibrations rolled through the house, Shirley shook, too, terrified that the lives of her daughter and husband may have already been sucked away into the diminishing sound. Whatever John had said, whatever her fears might have been, nothing could have prepared her for such a sudden and complete sense of loss. Gripping Simon tight to her she waited for the agony to go away. No other noise came. Then, a few feet away, Jack's thick-featured face suddenly glowed in the light of a match and he looked down at the boy.

'What's your name?' The voice was thick as tar.

The boy stared back. 'Simon.'

'I'm Jack. We're in a bit of a pickle, you and your Mum and me. We're going to have to stay down here for a few days, together ...' He extinguished the almost burned-out match by rolling it between finger and thumb. Another one was struck. 'First of all we need some candles. I know I chucked some down here. Do you know where they went?'

As they began to hunt among the household clutter, the words sank in. Would they really be all locked in here together for days on end, for weeks, for ever? When the second match burnt down, they were left searching blindly and Shirley immediately felt disorientated. Among the chaos of the damp cellar she did not dare step in any direction and the sensory loss combined with the feeling of real loss in her life to make her shiver fitfully. Then a warm breath, tinged with tobacco, blew over her face and a hand brushed her left thigh. It was impossible to know if it were chance or design. When a third match was lit and touched to a candle Jack had finally found, his face was impassive and Shirley could still not be sure. At that moment something distracted him and he looked round sharply, sniffing the air. Handing the candle to Shirley he walked to the bottom of the steps and sniffed pensively.

'I thought I turned everything off. Have you got anything electrical plugged in up there I might have missed? Heaters? Record player?'

Shirley tried to think, imagining each room in the house. 'There's a television in the bedroom.'

'Oh, Jesus.' He pounded up the stairs and went out through the door.

4: PITY ME

As the tyres of the pale green Rover burred and squealed through the country roads of Weardale towards Bishop Auckland, Dr MacGilvray's thick fingers jabbed at the buttons and twiddled at the tuner of the car radio in search of some news. In his anxiety to find so much as a crackle, he concentrated on the matter a few seconds too long and when he looked up he was nearly into a sharp right-hand bend he had not expected quite yet. The car fought against the breaks like a fish on a line, flailing first one way, then the other until it finally flew round one hundred and eighty degrees and brought two wheels to rest in the grass. The adrenalin pumped through him and he drew several deep breaths; that was the last thing he needed now. Starting off again, he took more care, abandoning the radio and keeping both hands on the wheel. Outside, at the windows of farms and villages, faces peeked from dark windows, dogs barked, and a cow bellowed her fear. Cars passed him in both directions, most travelling at least at the speed he had been before the spin. By the roadside some were parked, their drivers staying where they were or roaming up banks and out over fields to see what they could see. By a gate where the road lay between fields, a man was sitting with his head in his hands and in a passing glimpse MacGilvray saw him look up with white eyes. As the road climbed he could make out a vast blanket of smoke rising from the north, towards Durham, and spreading out into the clear blue sky. It was hard to know what factory, what gas or oil installation could have caused an explosion so large that it was beginning to take on the shape of a nuclear mushroom cloud.

It was nearly fifteen minutes after he had first seen the flash that he turned left on to the A688 and headed north towards Bishop Auckland. The main street straight ahead that led into the town was blocked by a white Durham Constabulary Cortina beside which two policemen were deep in conversation with a small group of women. The Rover turned right immediately in front of them to follow the road that skirted the town and the policemen looked up sharply. The explosion had come from further north, nearer home, and that was where the doctor was anxious to be. Passing by the Territorial Army centre, his attention was suddenly diverted by the sight of a Sedgefield councillor who a year back had sat on an Environmental Health and Control Committee with him. Curiosity caused him to slow down. Maggie Blackett was standing outside the building having a lively argument with someone he couldn't see. The curiosity, however, was no more than passing, and the automatic gears changed down to take him away over Coundon Burn and up the short hill that led to Spennymoor and Durham. Here the road narrowed to a single lane of traffic controlled by lights at each end. But there were no lights now and, as a consequence, a car and a van were locked together in splinters of metal and glass at the far end. It was then that Dr MacGilvray turned back into town to talk to the police.

When he passed the TAVR building again, Maggie Blackett was no longer at its door, but running along the road, her stride ungainly and her grey-streaked hair bouncing free. The sound of the car made her look over her shoulder and the doctor had little option but to draw up beside her. Immediately, she ran round to the passenger door, imagining it was an offer of a lift, and climbed in slamming the door hard. Either nerves or anger made her eyes bright and her thin, lined face was taut.

'What on earth's going on?'

'They won't tell us.'

'Who?' The car moved off again.

'The TA.'

'What's it to do with them?'

She squared up to him as if his ignorance was an offence. 'Didn't you hear the news?'

'I've been fishing. My radio's not working ...'

'It's nuclear, doctor. They've dropped a bomb on us.'

Involuntarily his right foot came up off the accelerator and when he spoke his words had slowed, too, the Highland vowels producing almost an incantation: 'Oh, Christ, it's finally happened.'

So that was why there had been a blind man on the road, and he had passed him by. He looked around, but there was no sign of the disaster, no planes or missiles streaking through the skies hemmed in by the buildings alongside the road. In a silence that was ominous the car drifted on to stop beside the road block. One of the policemen was immediately leaning over them. He could tell them nothing except what his orders were. He was adamant: they could not go on past the town; they must find somewhere to take shelter. And when MacGilvray explained he was a doctor he was told that all medical staff should report to the General Hospital just up the road. Ambulances, he said, had left to search for casualties and already more than a dozen had been brought in from the hillsides, their eyes scorched out by the flash. The councillor introduced herself. She was polite but firm. 'I'm one of Sedgefield's three Emergency Committee members and we're setting up the district council's War Headquarters in Spennymoor. We've asked the doctor to advise us on medical matters.'

They were too old, too respectable to be anything other than what they said they were. All the same, the policeman went to consult his colleague while they waited, not speaking for fear that overheard words might spoil their white lie. In the end the policeman flagged down a Fiesta that was touring the town with a megaphone telling people to stay where they were. This was their escort through the town.

It was a strange experience to drive along the main shopping street, the gloomy windows and fronts providing a slim barricade for the population of the town. It could have been no easy task for either the inhabitants or the police to clear the streets and, although there were undoubtedly stragglers around as there had been on the country roads, everyone was remarkably well rounded up. They might not have been so ordered if it had been a Thursday or Saturday when the market place just to the west of the Bishop's Palace would have been full of shoppers and stalls. All these people, all this organisation in just one town, a town like many others the length and breadth of the country, held in their complete silence a sense of foreboding, a sense that although a bomb had dropped, its full terror was yet to be released, a terror which would leave nobody unscarred. Patiently, in their hiding places, there was nothing anybody could do but wait. Their turn would undoubtedly come.

Sensing the unease, Maggie said: 'If these things are going off all over Britain, we won't have a chance. But I can't understand it. There was no warning, no build-up, nothing in the papers this morning.'

'Why here, though? There aren't any targets or military bases. There's just us – ordinary people. Don't you know anything? What about this committee, are you really on it?'

'No. I think there's meant to be one, though. There was a meeting last year about civil defence, but I couldn't make it.'

'So who's supposed to organise the rescue parties?'

'The army. Something called the UK Land Forces. The top brass will be in miles of bunkers around Salisbury Plain. We're in section 11 here. We've got our own special general tucked up in a bunker at Ouston, just outside Newcastle. The civilian government takes over a few weeks after the attack, with a junior minister appointed by Royal Warrant but I imagine Her Majesty's had other things on her mind in the past half hour. Then there's the County Council War Headquarters run by an Emergency Planning Officer up at Aykley Heads.'

The doctor glanced at her, thinking of the vast council offices in the north of Durham, a little more than a stone's throw from his own hospital where his colleagues would be. It wasn't long ago that the city had followed Newcastle in signing the Manchester Agreement, refusing to have nuclear weapons in its boundaries.

'Have you got family in town?'

'No.' He pursed his lips. 'Just very good friends.'

They had passed Auckland Park and reached a road block which stopped traffic leaving or entering Bishop from the north-east. Their escort explained the situation to a pipe-smoking sergeant and while a car moved back to let them through he came over to them.

'Hello, doctor.' They had seen each other around hospitals on more than one occasion before. 'I can't tell you anything that'll help. We're getting no information through at all. It looks like Durham, but what else I don't know. You can't see this radiation, you understand. That's really what we're most concerned about. So you go carefully, will you?'

Like millions of others he would have liked to have been doing more than just sitting tight. At least the doctor and the councillor had, until now, a degree of freedom which they might be able to use. Confirmation that the smoke he had seen was coming from Durham compounded Dr MacGilvray's desire to be doing all he could and he turned the car swiftly on to the A688 once more and headed up towards Spennymoor, the city and the ever blackening sky. As the cloud's size increased he thought of the fearful problems lying ahead. Many years ago he had read an account of Hiroshima. How many doctors had survived the bomb to help the hundreds of thousands in that city then? Was it five? Maybe seven. And how many hospital beds were there in Britain which could take care of patients with third-degree burns? A thousand, perhaps two at the very most. There would be many other kinds of casualties, too. And other bombs might have dropped or be on the way.

'Right here, turn right here,' Maggie suddenly burst in on his calculations as an ambulance sped by them going back to Bishop.

They were about a mile along the road and Dr MacGilvray had swung the car to the right before he knew why he was doing it. In a few moments they were climbing up the hill towards the scattered farms and houses of Westerton where, outside a house up for sale, they were greeted by a shaggy yapping dog. Bit by bit, as they rose, the scene to the left opened up to them. Dark clouds flecked with firefly sparks were gathered in a pillar a mile wide reaching upwards and spreading out so that nowhere within a ninety degree arc of vision was there anything but deathly grey. Dr MacGilvray stopped the car to take the scene in.

Hilltops of crayon-box spring green which swayed in the wind to show their shapes and colours in a hundred different ways looked now no more than slag heaps. Nature had been choked to death. The view was a vast crematorium of acre upon acre of burned-out crops and hedgerows, wildlife, sheep and cattle. Smoke puffed from black pinheads of trees, billowed from barns and houses and hovered amid spouts of flames above villages and towns where industrial estates, carefully concealed by planners, now showed themselves in gobbets of orange and red. For those in the two, perhaps three, coal mines beneath, suffocation would have been certain, if the tremors from the blast had not caved in the pits first. To the right, thin banners of black rose from the hidden motorway where tankers or chemical lorries burned. Nearer to them electricity pylons were twisted, their lines down, and the communications towers at Lanchester and Sunnyside were not to be seen. With the blanket of smoke, it was impossible to tell how far north the catastrophe spread, but at the near side of the central pall, some eight miles away, the greatest flames flew from the heart of the County Palatine.

Wrapped in the folds of the valleys and steep banks of the River Wear which entered the city from the south, looped back round the mixed and massive piles of the Norman cathedral and castle almost in an oxbow before leaving for the north and the west, Durham should have been largely protected from all but the closest or most massive blasts. But there was no telling what had caused the city to ignite and continue to burn, and even at this distance Maggie and Dr MacGilvray could sense the heat as they sat inside the car. Around them, trees rustled their leaves to let through the eager wind that was hurrying to feed the insatiable appetite of the flames. The two of them, sitting up there, felt as insignificant as a coal nut in the Eastham colliery, two people among 100,000 – or nearly half a million if the disaster had crossed the Tyne and ravaged Newcastle too. Any one of the fires on the hillsides, any one of the factories or warehouses now in flames would normally have demanded half the county's emergency services. Now, in the core of the furnace, many of these services would themselves be in need of all the help in the world. Exposed on the high ground to the north of the city were the quarter-million square feet of modern council offices, the constabulary and fire brigade headquarters, the main hospital where MacGilvray worked, an electricity transmission station and a sewage works, all scattered over the high land around Aykley Heads, Framwell Moor and Pity Me.

Stunned by the sight, the two sat immobile, watching, each trying to work out just how extensive the damage was, each unable to cast from their minds the suffering of those they knew and didn't know. The picture they saw was bad enough, the ones their minds painted were far worse.

After a few minutes Maggie said quietly, 'We'll have to know what the radiation level is. I think one of the underground monitoring posts is somewhere near here. Perhaps we could try to find it ...'

'Bugger that, let's get down there.' The engine started up and they reversed into a gateway.

'But they might be in touch with London ... or Salisbury Plain ...'

'Look.'

She followed the direction of his outstretched arm, towards the fields over to the south. Squinting, she could just make out the smudge on the horizon, the vignette of grey. It could have been coming from anywhere between there and London 250 miles to the south. Maggie tightened her seat belt as the car roared away.

5: UNDERGROUND

Rosamund was nearly beaten. Her hooves clopped unsteadily, sometimes stopping briefly, sometimes stumbling on the tarmac path beside the stiff, dark fibres which had not long before had been emerald-rich spring grass. Her right eye was covered with a thin film, evidence that her sight was damaged. Now and then she did not even know how far away the ground was. Her mane was wild and greased as if she had not been combed in weeks and her chestnut flanks, dark with sweat, were peppered with small black patches like cigarette burns on a carpet. She barely responded to the occasional loose flick on her reins or to the murmured words of comfort from her rider.

When the first flash had occurred she had been nudging at a clump of people gathered on the eastern pavement beneath Admiralty Arch. The police officer on her back was urging her to squeeze them in, hoping to make space for themselves. But when the light seared through the sky Rosamund had reared and kicked out violently, smashing her legs against the stones and ploughing her iron shoes into screaming human flesh. She was still bucking when the explosion drove her wild and it was only the confines of the space that prevented her from bolting. Then, when Nelson's column toppled over, cutting down across the cars and hurling the Admiral's body at the feet of Uganda House, she pulled backwards, found space and made off down the Mall, only to meet with the scorching trees. Hurled about like a rodeo rider, the officer was one minute down on her neck and the next his own was nearly snapped as he whiplashed back. More through luck than through his considerable experience he managed to hold on until she tired and they both felt the rumpus could go on no more.

Neither of them the victor in the fight, they now wandered through the charred landscape down the pathway in St James's Park that ran beside Horse Guards Road. The policeman, hatless, rocked unsteadily in the saddle. There were blisters on his palms, and his eyes and mouth and half his face was swollen. Though his muscles ached he could not single out a part of him that had been injured. He just felt tired and rather sick. On both horse and rider there had begun to appear gobbets of thick, black rain.

Beside them the trees, which earlier that day had carried bouquets of pink and white blossom and small green buds of life, were now smouldering sticks and the clear view across the park was of a lunar landscape in monochrome. On the lake's Duck Island a greylag goose honked dolefully and beside the water a ruffled mother duck with three chicks dead beside her could only blink to show that she was alive. The few people who were in the park were also grey, colourless ghosts on the moonscape. Of those who were prostrate it was impossible to tell who was living, who was injured, who was just petrified or praying. One or two were wandering aimlessly, perhaps among them those who had come to the park to die and had been cheated, and were now wondering why they still drew breath, why they had been misled. They did not yet know that this was not a full nuclear strike or that the holocaust had been caused by a single, unexpected weapon.

Irritated by the smoke that billowed from the fires to the north and east, filling the thick air with dust and ashes, Rosamund's nostrils occasionally fluttered and it was this sound that Tel first heard when, fifty yards away in the shelter of the Leafpound, he raised his head from the earth he had been thrown in. Immediately, he was shaken by a dreadful disorientation. None of the surroundings were familiar: the smouldering hut, the burned-out rubbish pile, the charcoal sticks that stood out on the bed of earth above the concrete wall around him. The sky was overcast and he thought it must be winter but he could not recall the sense of it. He had no jacket and his shoes were gone. What could have possessed him to leave home in this weather wearing just a sweatshirt? But where was home? Oh, Jesus, it wasn't a difficult question. Where did he come from?

Shakily, he got to his feet, brushing off the handfuls of earth that had fallen on him as they might have fallen on a coffin from mourners' hands. Nothing was broken; his body seemed intact. Here he was, an alien in a foreign land. He slammed a hand against the concrete. 'You stupid, bloody walls, where are you?' And his voice choked against the sobs. For a moment he stood, breathing deeply, telling himself to get a grip. Then, nervous of what he might find, he began to look for clues, walking with deliberate steps in his stockinged feet, past a tractor and two mesh-boxed trailers, past a roofless, blackened hut and, following the compound round to the left, found himself out in the park again beside the shattered, paint-stripped cars in Birdcage Walk – and something, somewhere seemed a little bit familiar. To his left, turning in his direction, came the phantom of the policeman and Rosamund and, if nothing else, Tel knew the man in uniform was not a welcome sight. He moved on the other way, cutting up towards the lake.

It was a monstrous dream, a piece of sorcery that had taken him over the abyss. He watched his feet press into the warm, prickly stubble of the grass and he wondered once again where he lived, where he, ... for the love of God, he could not even remember his name. What was it, what was it? A sob came again. As he neared the water his eyes fixed on a figure sitting on the ground, knees drawn up, shoulders hunched, a streak of red in the close-cropped blonde hair. She watched him approach from the corner of her eye and he was sure he knew her. Reaching her, he saw the sad look on her soft face but she did not greet him like a friend.

'Scuse me,' he said quietly. 'Can I sit down with you? I don't think I'm mad but my head's not right and I don't know what's going on.'

Her smile was tight but not unkind. And Tel noticed that a patch on her right cheek was no longer covered by any flesh. He felt sick and for a long time they sat together looking silently at the lifeless water.

'There was this geezer who goes to the doctor one morning and the doctor tells him he's got just twenty-four hours to live . . .'

At last, thought Beat. The prospect of a joke, however old or boring, was like a blast of common sense. The voice, coming from some way away beneath the floor, wasn't easy to hear and, although she could not be sure it seemed as if it belonged to somebody who was not entirely sober. It had been some minutes since Alan had stopped his manic fling beneath the basement of what had been Pennines Assurance and the sound of falling earth had vanished into silence. This new voice had brought an end to their waiting. Beat smiled and Jeffrey saw it.

'You're not going down there, are you?' He was standing close, his heavy body heaving with the effort of breathing. Everything seemed to be closing in: from the partly demolished building above them to the darkness that beckoned beyond the candle's glow.

'Why not?'

'But it's a pit. Once you're in, there's no way of knowing you're going to get out. We could stick it out up here.'

'It's getting very warm. At least the air down there might be moving.' Beat was actually dripping, dark ovals were creeping out from beneath her armpits and the white cotton blouse was prickly on her back. Round her slightly owly face dark hair curled in damp ringlets and her usually sparkling clear brown eyes were dulled. Jeffrey couldn't claim to feel much better. Already his tie was loosened and beads of water speckled his pale skin from his forehead back up over his bare head, gleaming in the light of the candle he held. The last thing Beat now wanted was to be stuck in a room with him again and, glancing at him, she knew they were both recalling what should have been their last minutes together. Any second, she thought, he's going to resurrect that moment as if it were still an event, as if it were part of a continuing, mutual emotion.

'Besides,' he said on cue, 'I've got some unfinished business.'

Beat looked at his lopsided leer, the kind that made secretaries yawn, and she wondered at the insensitivity that kept him going. She could have said, 'Really? I thought you were quite satisfied,' but she saved her breath.

Alan's voice broke in, echoing loudly up from the black hole below. 'Whoever's coming first, bring the box of candles.'

'Bossy sod,' said Jeffrey.

'They're over there,' Beat pointed.

'You, too, darling.' He brought the box over to the hole. 'It's okay, you go first, I'll take it. I'm not staying here alone with some old boiler. You get down there, I'll be right behind. But afore ye go …'

He reached his hand out and placed it behind her head, trying to bring her face towards his for a kiss. Beat pulled away. Kissing, she had always understood, was what two people did when they both felt like it.

Stepping into the hole her low-heeled shoes pressed into the earth, checking its firmness and, bending low, she squinted in the direction Alan had taken. It was dark as death and she had to suppress the thought that Jeffrey might be right: from the frying pan they may be crawling slowly and inevitably into the fire.

Alan's instructions were brisk. 'You come along about fifteen feet, but you'll have to go on your belly. Don't touch the sides, they might fall in. After that it drops a couple of feet into a small tunnel. You should be all right there.'

Beat was undecided how to go. If anything was going to fall down on her she didn't want it in the face. And if anything caved in, she would rather her lower half knew about it first. So she lay down on her stomach, clutching her handbag, and began to wriggle down into the cavity. She had gone no more than a couple of yards when she saw the flaw in her reasoning. Shuffling backwards on her elbows, particles of dust raining down on her, she felt her calf-length skirt ride up, exposing first her shins, then her knees and thighs to cuts from the protruding bricks and jagged chunks of mortar. To overcome the scratches she raised each leg carefully as she moved and she remembered swimming lessons years ago in Bromley baths. The movement strained the muscles now even more than it had pulled at them when she was a plump child. Finally, after ten painfully slow minutes, she dropped down into the still-standing segment of the tunnel where the going was easier, and it wasn't long before she was kicking air.

A pair of hands grabbed each ankle but instead of easing her down she heard an unfamiliar voice say: 'Hang on.' Then, as an aside: 'We need your waistcoat.' There was the sound of material being torn and she felt cloth being wound around her ankles. When Beat asked what they were doing, the same voice went on matter-of-factly: 'Just giving you some protection from the rats.' She shivered. 'Normally you'd recover from a bite - if you got to a hospital within twenty-four hours. But public services are going to be a bit overcrowded and lots of doctors may be dead.'

Beat almost laughed at the man's appalling bedside manner when the hands began to guide her naked legs down into the thin layer of mire. The moment she slipped into it, she knew this was a sewer. The smell, the dank yellowing bricks, the small flame of a lighter, made it seem like a nineteenth-century Gothic horror and she thought of Jack the Ripper. In the middle of the tunnel, running down its centre, was a dry path and it was on this that the short, plump young man with the lighter stood grinning. Even if he had not been carrying a bottle she would have picked him out as the comedian. The other stranger, the one who had been so cheerful about the rats, was no taller, but his bearded face was pinched and more worried-looking than his bald statements of the awaiting horrors had suggested.

From the tunnel a fresh scuffling sound heralded Jeffrey's arrival but Alan had stepped forward, a courteous and silent chaperone, to take Beat's arm and guide her to the dry centre aisle. So he was not at the small tunnel's entrance to tell his colleague to stop while they bandaged up his ankles as they had done Beat's. Instead he arrived with a leap on to the floor, and a smattering of excrement.

'Where are the candles?' was all that Alan wanted to know.

'Christ, it's really rank in here.' Jeffrey brought the box down from the hole above him while John explained about the protective material for the legs. Jeffrey refused to rip up any of his clothes and compromised by just tucking his trousers into his socks. Alan took the box from him, lit a candle and handed it to John. By its light the blueing bruises and the dark scrapes of blood showed on the hands that had toiled so feverishly.

'You'd better cover those up,' said John.

'They'll be all right.' They were the least of Alan's worries.

'They might be now but there's so much disease in this

place they'll be infected very quickly.' He helped Alan tear the tails of his Turnbull and Asser shirt up into strips. 'The men who work down here get very sick for the first couple of weeks,' he said encouragingly. 'After that they don't know a day's illness in their lives. They seem to get the lot at once, and then they are immune.'

'Well, that's something to look forward to then,' said Alan.

From beside her, above the thick odour that was creeping into her stomach, Beat caught a whiff of scotch.

'I thought it was always meant to be the women who tore up their blouses and petticoats at a time like this,' said Bob.

Beat smiled. 'Petticoats are out of fashion.'

'I know,' said Bob, 'I peeked.'

She was glad of the new company, someone who would not remind her of her immediate past each time she looked at him. 'I'm Beat,' she said.

'Don't worry, love, beneath this flabby frame there's a Mr Universe aching to get out. I'll carry you if you like.'

'No,' she explained. 'Beat, short for Beatrix, that's my name.'

'Oh, pardon me. I'm Bob. Have a drink.'

Alcohol usually gave her a headache very quickly and most of the time she avoided it, but to be friendly she put the bottle to her lips and let a dribble burn round her mouth. It might also, she hoped, chase a few germs away. John had begun to explain their situation, that the sounds of tunnels falling in had seemed to come from the east, that that was the way the wind, now a flickering breeze that made the candle flames bob and duck, had headed and they had no choice but to go west. Beat's home, a cottage near Colchester where she had lived alone since her divorce three years ago, was in the other direction, but if what this man said was right, then there was no point in trying to get there now. She wondered if she would see it again: the books, the country kitchen, the black cat called Bo Diddley. In the garden this year were going to be raspberries, courgettes, marrows, as well as beans and peas and broccoli. Next week a builder was coming to fix the leak in the roof which she had been meaning to have done for ages. She thought of all these things without bitterness but with resignation.

They had begun moving off, John and Alan out in front, John with a candle in one hand, the briefcase in the other, Alan unable to grip a thing in his bound-up hands. A few yards behind them came the other three, led by Jeffrey's glimmering light. Refusing to carry the bulky box, he had stuffed the candles in his jacket and trouser pockets which now bulged, making him a shadow of a cartoon fat man waddling along the gloomy path of bricks.

'This stink's really getting to my gut,' he complained.

'When you're in a city of seven million frightened people,' Bob philosophised, 'the last place you want to be is in a sewer.'

'They certainly caught us with our trousers down,' said Jeffrey. 'The bastards. I hope that whatever else our boys are up to now they're pressing all the buttons and making sure the Russians get well and truly nuked.'

'I expect they are, Jeffrey,' said Beat with none of his enthusiasm.

'Well, they can't be far away,' said Bob. 'The government. I bet their little hidey-hole doesn't stink like this. Hey, General!' His voice echoed down the tunnel and a rat scooted into the light beside him. Its tail seemed nearly a foot long. 'Where's the place the bigwigs are hanging out in? Can we pop in for a wash and tidy up?'

'The next citadel we pass is on our left,' replied John, the ever-helpful guide. 'Under Horseferry Road.'

'Blimey, I've just been there. I bet that magistrate's tucked up nice and cosy somewhere. He looked the kind of sly fox who'd always have a hole to crawl into ... ooops!'

Mistaking a solid lump of cooking fat for a slab of concrete Bob had slipped into the film of sludge beside the path. 'Ooo-er!' he complained, fumbling for the bottle to make sure it wasn't broken. Only a small drop had spilled out. Beat pulled at his arm and helped him to his unsteady feet. His left side was damp and smelly.

'Here,' Beat took a bottle of perfume from her handbag and handed it to him. 'You might as well come up smelling of roses.'

'Ta, you're a gent.' Bob sprinkled the liquid over his head and clothes liberally but it only had a temporary effect.

For a seeming age they stumbled onwards, each step falling carefully on the uneven path as they listened to the rustling of the rats. By now they were growing used to the small flickering lights and the appalling smell, though none of them were feeling well on it. If there was any kind of claustrophobia it was lessened by the knowledge that outside there was unlikely to be any fresh air, that there would be fires and radiation and there would be inescapable scenes of suffering. However uncomfortable they were, they knew it could have been worse. Much worse.

The cuts on Beat's legs still stung like pin pricks and she continually squeezed the cloth of her skirt against them to soothe them as she walked. Beside her, Bob had become less talkative, putting his concentration into trying to stay upright. He was rather drunk.

'What happened to the man who went to the doctor?' she asked to keep him talking.

'Mmm? What man?'

'The one who only had twenty-four hours to live.'

'Oh, *that* man.' Bob perked up, determinedly forcing back the slur that had sneaked into his voice. 'Well, he collars his best mate and tells him: "Look, I've just been told I've only got twenty-four hours to live. I'm going to take all my money out of the bank and we're going on the biggest bender you ever had ..."'

'That's an old one,' Jeffrey said churlishly.

Bob wasn't put off. 'I was talking to the lady ... So they started off at lunchtime at the cocktail bar at the Hilton. And for three hours they went through the menu: tequila and salad, crême de menthe and salad, curaçao and salad, wallbangers, headbangers, slow screws . . .'

'Hold it!' John and Alan had stopped up ahead.

'... fast screws ...'

'What is it?' Jeffrey asked.

'Cave-in.'

'Shit.'

They gathered by the heap of bricks that sloped forwards up to the ceiling, a solid wall that sat there like a boulder at the exit of a tomb.

'Can we get past?' Jeffrey asked.

John was examining the fall, clambering gingerly over the lower bricks and letting candlelight rove among the mess. As usual he did not speak until he had something to say, and he found nothing to speak of until he settled on a spot about five feet from the ground and as many back where the flame flickered wildly, dancing his exaggerated shadow above them round the ceiling.

'Air's still getting through. There is a hole but we will have to be careful.'

He stood up, his hair brushing the ceiling, and the others waited for him to come to a decision. Then, gently, he began taking bricks from around the spot where the air was coming from, handing them backwards, without looking round. Alan passed them on to Jeffrey who gave them to Bob.

'And when they had finished the cocktails,' Bob continued as the brick-clearing chain fell into a routine, 'they moved on to Shepherd's Market where they booked two girls for the afternoon. Everything. They tried everything. Well, they had to in a way, 'cos they were so full of cocktails. This bloke was really anxious he shouldn't snuff it without having tried it all – custard pies, feather dusters, I don't know ...'

'Whips and leather gear?' Jeffrey offered.

Bob looked at Beat and they both managed to say together in mock surprise: 'Whips and leather gear, aye?'

But their laughter was drowned by the pounding of bricks that rained down from the pile. John managed to jump clear as nimbly as a scree runner, grabbing Alan in his stride and dragging him to safety. Beat looked at Alan, then at Jeffrey whose face was ashen. He was staring straight ahead. She followed his gaze and saw, just revealed high up the fallen wall where John had been working, a few inches of leg, a dark sock hanging half off the foot.

'Oh God,' said Jeffrey.

The others saw what he was looking at and felt the same sense, a closeness of death. There was no telling if there were others, only a few yards from them, trapped beneath the bricks. Perhaps they had been like themselves, a hopeless bunch looking for nothing more than shelter and a chance to live. John climbed tentatively up towards the limb and when he reached it he hesitated, then he pinched it sharply. There was no response. 'We can't pull him out,' he said flatly. 'Otherwise the whole lot will come down. Pass me up some bricks.'

Alan did so and the chain worked in reverse as John began to stack the bricks up around the leg until it was covered. Climbing back down again, he looked up from his careful steps and realised everyone's eyes were on him. He shrugged his shoulders. 'I think, really, that that's that.' His disappointment showed.

'There was a large pipe leading off to the right about fifty yards back,' Jeffrey said. 'Perhaps we could get out through that.'

John looked at his watch. 'It's best if we stay down here another eighteen hours. If we can. The worst of the initial fall-out should be over by then. I suppose I was being a bit optimistic thinking these old tunnels would still be standing all the way to Hammersmith.'

A feeling of impotence fell on all of them. However much they detested the place they were in, at least they had been kept going by the knowledge it was leading somewhere. Now they saw themselves, bedraggled, hot, stinking, their clothes in tatters and the figure of John before them, the person they had relied on to lead them, no more than a sorry small person, like themselves. He sighed as he found himself a place to sit among the bricks. Bob handed him the bottle and Alan sat beside him.

'Cheer up, General,' said Bob. 'We'll all be smelling of roses this time tomorrow.'

But his words were lost. John was thinking of home: so near, as the song said, yet so far away.

There was a fire in the house. Shirley could smell it now. Not long after Jack had left the cellar he had called down to ask if there was a hose in the garden. There was, and he went to fetch it. Shirley listened to him go out of the back door, waited for his returning footsteps and heard the water cascade through the house above. It made it difficult to concentrate on her most important task: keeping Simon happy. Her own nervousness was not helping him to settle and she tried hard to conceal it, organising a game of 'making house', tidying the shambles of the cared-for possessions she and John had so carefully chosen, so meticulously kept, putting them in the 'larders' and 'fridges' of the knocked about drawers. Each time the boy was occupied for more than a second she would think again of Jenny and John, wondering if the phones might be working, if it was worth trying to give the office or the school a ring. Could she risk scurrying to Jenny's school to see if she were safe? Simon couldn't come with her, nor could he stay here. She only hoped Jack was all right. Whatever else she thought of him, there might already be good cause to be thankful he had walked into her life.

It was more than an hour after he had left in such a fury that Jack returned, coming through the door with a wastepaper basket full of water in each hand. As he descended the steps the light from the candle made deep shadows move over his arms and legs where the muscles showed. Shirley watched them distractedly keeping her eyes on his thighs and calfs as they rose and fell, not immediately registering what she was witnessing. With some embarrassment she realised that by avoiding his eyes she had been staring at his body. His hair was drenched and he wore nothing but his underclothes.

'What's happened?' she asked hurriedly.

He carried the wastepaper baskets over to the old laundry tub and emptied the water into it.

'Afraid your bedroom's a bit wet. It was half alight when I got there. Your curtains and bedding's gone. These things give a rush of power through your electrics and your appliances blow up. I got this water out of your expansion tank, though. Should be fresh. I'll get some more later.'

'But where are your clothes?'

He looked down at himself and frowned, as if his state of undress had only just occurred to him and, despite his evident maturity, Shirley was reminded of a small boy being told he had mud on his Sunday suit.

'Oh, they're upstairs.' He didn't seem bothered. 'That fallout, or whatever it is, it's coming down like black snow. I thought I'd better not bring it in here. Gave the barnet a wash and all. Have you got a radio?'

There was a small portable inside a drawer. She took it out and handed it to him, her arm straight, not getting too close. It wasn't working and he carried it to the back of the cellar where Shirley had set the candle down. When he asked for a screwdriver it was Simon who knew where it was. Jack began to dismantle the portable.

'Where's your husband work?'

'Westminster.'

'What was he, civil servant?'

'He *is* a civil servant.'

Jack looked up, startled at the sudden vehemence. 'Sorry, just a manner of speaking.'

'And he's very clever. He's good at ... surviving. He walks a lot. We go camping sometimes, with the children. Box Hill, Leith Hill. He knows all the trees and flowers ...'

Jack didn't seem to be listening. The back fell off the radio and clattered on to the concrete floor. As he picked it up he said: 'Did you say your daughter was at school?'

'Yes. Brackenbury.'

He nodded.

'I thought ... I want to find out if she's all right.'

He kept nodding. It irritated her.

'Could I leave Simon with you while I went to see? It's not far.'

His head changed direction and began to shake. 'That stuff I got all over my clothes, I don't think it does anybody any good. Probably gives you leukaemia or something. Leave it a while and we'll see what happens. From what I could tell in the garden, damage round here's only superficial, windows and that. Brackenbury's a solid old school and they must have got the warning. They should be all right.' He looked up to see her doubt. 'When it's cleared a bit I'll go and have a look for you. You stay here with the kid.'

The distracted expression on his face dissolved into a smile. Then the door burst open.

'Aha, you thought you could hide, did you? Thought you could get away this time in your secret tunnels with your harlots and your drink.'

Jack flew at the meths drinker, rushing the stairs two at a time. But as he neared the top the old man hurled himself forwards, catching Jack off balance, and together they crashed in a storm of dust down the stairs. In one movement Shirley scooped Simon up and leapt to the far corner of the room where Jack had been sitting. Squatting there with her arms hiding the sight from her son, it seemed that the full aggression of the world had entered her home, found her last hiding place and was now crying for blood at her feet. In the candlelight she made out the intruder's face, old and lined and spiked with greying stubble, folds of baggy flesh under his watery eyes, and she knew he was as mad as the men who had launched the nuclear attack. It could have only been madness that made a man of his age and dissipation fight with such fury, an equal match for the labourer who appeared twice his size.

'Where's Daddy? Where's Daddy?' the boy suddenly wanted to know.

'Hush, Simon. He's at work today.'

'Why are those men fighting? Don't they like each other?'

'Hush now.' She tried to keep her voice calm. Cold as a night dew, she watched the two men who, for a while were locked together, the old man growling as if there were a hand at his throat. Then the entwined figures blew apart and in an instant the old man was thrown against the wall, falling down beside her. There was spittle on his chin and his pale eyes were wild.

'What did you do to get yourself a place here?' he spat, 'you with your bastard child.'

Shirley hardly knew she had the screwdriver in her hand, hardly knew she had lashed out, splitting his cheek. But as the instrument went deeper, slowed first by something spongy then checked by more solid matter, and as the blood pumped across her tightly-clenched fist, she knew she had done it. She had joined in the violence that was ending the world. And Simon had seen it, too. She put an arm round him, careful not to paint him with any blood. Beside them the drunk was silent, the screwdriver handle against his cheek, and it was hard to know if he were still living. Jack didn't seem to mind either way. He picked the old man up, turned him round and pulled his shoulderblades down across his knees. There was a small 'crack' when he jerked the head back. The body fell to the floor and he stood for a moment, narrow-eyed and breathing deeply.

Then he turned to her. 'Well done. Got any bin liners?'

'What?' He might as well have been speaking Greek.

'Dustbin liners. Big black ones.'

'I'll get them.' Before she could stop him, Simon had pulled away from her and run helpfully across the room where he produced a roll tied up with string.

'Did you kill him?' he wanted to know, in the same way he might have asked if he had been to the shops.

Jack grinned. 'No. I just gave him a headache.'

'What are you going to do with him?'

'I'm going to wrap him up like a parcel and then I'm going to send him home for his Mum to look after.'

He took two bags from the roll, pulling one over the corpse's head, the other up over its feet. Then he slung it over his shoulder and climbed the stairs. Shirley listened to the weighty footsteps on the hallway floor above, to the front door being opened. She shivered violently and the muscles round her stomach pulled like cords of ice. Then she was sick.

6: SPENNYMOOR

The life of a mine, it's said, begins to fade the moment the first lump of coal is taken from it. In Spennymoor, six miles south of Durham, the discovery of coal brought the once small rural village such industry that when its ironworks opened there in 1892 they were the largest in the world. But when the seams thinned and expired and the collieries closed down, the town was not allowed to die too. Light industry was brought in, planned and encouraged and tidied away on two estates beyond the houses, and the population settled at around 20,000. Now the town had a modern sports centre and a shopping precinct, where the Salvation Army sometimes preached and played. To the north, up towards Mount Pleasant, was the Green Lane Industrial Estate where the largest factory produced power tools. On the Trading Estate, on the east side of the A688, the biggest company was a domestic appliance and light manufacturers who employed more than 8000 people. To house the staff of these companies, a large estate of grey-textured concrete squares and rows, rising from one to five storeys tall, had been built at Bessemer Park beside the road through to Durham at the north end of the town. Not as unsightly as many, it was peppered with squares of grass and beside it was a full-sized football pitch. It had, nevertheless, not escaped the afflictions of programmed housing as the smashed windows of three or four unoccupied units showed.

It was because many of those who lived in Spennymoor worked close to home that most had been able to return to their families when the warning had sounded, though not without some confusion and panic when the bolt of light whipped over their heads and the blast shook the ground beneath their feet. Some windows and shop fronts had shattered, causing cuts, loose tiles had slipped from roofs and more than one puffing chimney pot had toppled over. The fires that broke out, mostly started by the surge of power through the electricity supply, were, through self-help, soon brought under control. There were larger fires, though, mostly up towards Mount Pleasant, and the town's two fire engines had more calls than they could manage. Even before the exodus from the north had begun to arrive, the police, with no radios or any idea of the extent of the blast, had a difficult task on their hands. If they had used the counters correctly – and there had been some debate – then the radiation level was just under 200 rads. According to their books such a dose meant that vomiting could occur and that within a few hours other symptoms such as nausea, dizziness, tiredness and loss of appetite would continue for about a day. There would also be a moderate fall in the white blood cell count. Since there was no cure for radiation sickness, the documents the police dug up stressed the need for reassurance. Unless complications occurred, such a dose was not considered to be fatal. Apart from dealing with the minor crises of small injuries and fire, the force's main occupation was keeping the bemused population indoors.

At the roundabout by the Bessemer estate, the doctor's Rover was forced to a final standstill some forty minutes after the blast. What had started as a road block beside the exit to the town, now looked like the scene of a multiple pile-up. Vehicles blocked the roundabout and choked the Durham exit where a bus had overturned. Cars, vans and lorries were parked or being directed by police and civilians with handkerchiefs or gauze masks on their faces, the human cargoes shifted about, some stretched out on the grass in the centre of the roundabout, their injuries quickly covered by blankets, others standing or sitting transfixed, or wandering in a daze. Following the example of the officers, Dr MacGilvray and Maggie Blackett put handkerchiefs to their noses and went swiftly over to the crowd. From among it a burly man, who looked more like a farmer than the detective he was, watched them approach. Maggie introduced him to Dr MacGilvray before he led them away to an unmarked car at the back of the road block.

Briefly he explained that more than a hundred casualties had already arrived from Durham and that ambulances from Bishop as well as some private cars had taken about thirty of them away. With GPs busy in their own practices with the town's casualties, which included several heart-attack cases, the only medical help on hand was being provided by two nurses employed on the industrial estate. He spoke like somebody who had just stepped from a car crash, as if each thing he said could find no reality to attach itself to, and all the while he looked around him, his eyes unable to settle on a single thing he saw.

'They'll be full down there soon,' the doctor said.

'I know. We're not sending any more off until we know they've got somewhere to go. There's two police motorcyclists out trying to find out what's going on. Anyway, we're not dealing with the worst cases, of course, only the ones likely to survive.'

'What?' The councillor sounded as if she had not heard what he said.

'You know the emergency rules, Maggie.'

'But not here, not now. Who's deciding who's going to live?'

'You can tell, just by looking at them. There have been some so badly burned it's a wonder they're still alive.'

'That's murder!'

'Don't shout at me, lass!' But it was he who was shouting. 'You take it up with the council. It's their decision.'

Maggie raised two placatory palms. 'All right, Barry, I'll do that. Could you take me up there?'

He started up the engine, and the car moved off. 'As you know, doctor, there's no hospital here, but there's a young locum over at the health centre. We've already taken a dozen or so of the casualties there, and the more in one place things are, the easier they are to manage.'

'All right.'

'We'll try to get anything you want.'

It didn't matter how well equipped the health centre was, it was going to need a cornucopia of supplies. MacGilvray reeled off a list to the inspector who frowned in concentration trying to remember it all. It wasn't just the items, it was the searching thought of just where they might be found. From the three chemists he needed drugs for vomiting and nausea, calcium tablets, antibiotics, painkillers, gauze bandages, raw alcohol. From elsewhere blankets, a continual supply of uncontaminated water, a stove to boil it on and a generator would have to be rigged up to provide light. And, if by any miracle the area health authority could find one to spare, a blood transfusion unit – 'with enough blood to fill the Wear'. The list was long and items kept occurring to the doctor, his voice flat with a note of defeat which he could not hide. They were all aware of the increasing size of the problems that stretched out in front of them. Like walking over the neighbouring hills, the conquering of any one of them only led to the sight of the next one to be climbed. Passing through the town, silent but for the police with their megaphones, the three of them looked at the buildings in a new light, wondering what each might provide. When the car drew up outside the health centre, the policeman promised to do all he could. Already some of the sources had been plundered.

'One other thing,' the doctor said, pausing a second as he swung his legs out of the car. He looked directly at the inspector. 'Bring them all over here. Don't leave anybody out in the road to catch cold.'

Then he slammed the door and ran up the few steps to the modern, angular, brown-brick one-storey building. Even before he went through the glass doors he could see the injured packed inside the hall. Saturday night in the Dryburn casualty didn't have a quarter the number of cases. Noting the extent of the cuts and burns that blackened and flayed the victims, he made his way through them, grunting non-commitally in answer to occasional questions. Helpers were comforting the victims but they could do little else. He went in through a door marked with the regular doctor's name. Over a couch stained with blood a middle-aged nurse and a young doctor were tinkering with a patient who had severe cuts down his right side and his face. They looked up as he came in.

'MacGilvray,' he announced. 'Consultant physician at the Dryburn. What can I do?'

The flush that came over the young doctor's cheeks could not have been caused simply by the older man being asked for orders from someone his junior. The two men had met somewhere before. 'Good to see you, sir. If you'd like to wash up, there's water over there.'

As the doctor scrubbed his hands of fish scales, he was thinking of the work in process. Taking glass splinters from that one patient could occupy a doctor for several hours. But how else could they work? Then he remembered where he had seen the young doctor before. A few years back he had been dragged from his bed to attend casualty where a young medical student had been brought in, rattling with pills, an attempted suicide.

Sedgefield lay eight miles south west of Spennymoor and though it gave its name to the local government district, its council was housed in the former Area Headquarters of the National Coal Board in Spennymoor. It was here that the district's 53 councillors regularly met, though there were no more than half a dozen in the building now. The full-time staff, however, were all fully occupied. The meeting chamber, with its large table to seat all the members, was now the centre of activity. This was where, according to Home Office guidelines, the district's War Headquarters should be and where a triumvirate should be organising the town. None had emerged. Instead, the doors were kept open and into the room had come anybody with something to offer, something to say, and decisions were taken as quickly as possible so that there should be no delays in coming to grips with the problems that were springing up all around them. As a result there were more than thirty people in the room: directors, works managers, union representatives, a bus inspector, bank manager, Bingo hall boss and Co-op chief buyer. The Post Office, gas and electricity boards were also represented. On the council side were two council depot employees, a librarian to supply maps and information and secretaries to do anything but make the tea. In the absence of telephones this gathering of people was constantly changing as requests and instructions were taken backwards and forwards, and a system of runners was developing which a union official had described as the 'pop-across men', volunteers who would dash about the town. It was into this chaos that Maggie Blackett stepped, asking the same question each had asked as they came through the door: 'What's going on?'

'Ah, Health and Environmental Control!' Councillor Greenhalgh was a small bird of a man with a George Formby squeak to his Durham accent.

Maggie nodded towards him and made her way directly over to a group surrounding the chief executive, Ted Evans, a man in his late forties who had lived in the town all his life. When she discovered nobody knew more than she did, she quickly explained how she had arrived with the doctor from Durham and when she mentioned their diversion up to Westerton, Ted Evans showed sudden interest and pushed her towards the table where maps were spread out. As well as she could remember it, she filled in the picture, pencilling in on an already heavily-marked Ordnance Survey the areas she thought had been damaged, where the smoke and the fire came from, where the hills and fields had turned from green to black.

While she spoke, the crisis whirled round them. The fire up on the Green Lane Industrial Estate was getting out of hand, other buildings would have to be evacuated. Another water main had burst. Why couldn't the Robinsons join the rest of their family in Bishop where the air would be safer to breathe? Where was the lorryload of tinned food just arrived to be put? Why wasn't there any news from the monitoring posts? Was there anything yet from the town's radio ham? Every now and then Evans would look up from the map to overhear a conversation or confirm a course of action another councillor had suggested was taken. When Maggie had finished making her marks and explaining how she saw the county's destruction, he studied the map for a moment, leaning over it, looking at the hills, the roads, the houses. It was about how they had imagined it: there was no doubt a lot of people would be coming their way.

'There's one other matter,' Maggie said. 'I understand there's a selection process going on among the survivors coming from Durham, and that it was a council decision to leave the worst of them where they are.'

'It's not quite like that. The police wanted to know what the priorities were, and we only had that government circular to fall back on.'

She took in a breath, pushing down her anger. 'But not

even the consultant physician could tell you who's going to live. He hasn't got a crystal ball.'

Greenhalgh appeared beside them with a loose-leaf folder open in his hands. He pointed to a paragraph: 'Here it is, Circular 77 (1): "Hospitals should take in only those casualties likely to be alive after seven days with a fair chance of eventual recovery." It's a clear directive. The Home Office doesn't just make these things up. They've gone into it. It's part of a co-ordinated plan ...'

'Like their plans for communications? How many circulars have you got there from the Home Office about communications after a nuclear attack? Six? And we can't even phone up a neighbour. We'd do better with carrier pigeons.'

'Now that's an idea.' Greenhalgh's face lit up.

'Don't be daft ...'

'They'd probably get picked up by Fylingdales,' someone interjected, 'and blown out of the sky by whatever's left of Britain's strike force.'

'What do you suggest, then,' Ted Evans asked, 'about the survivors?'

Maggie gazed at the map for a moment, then she looked up. 'Councillor Greenhalgh's right,' she said. 'We should follow the instructions and get the least injured off to hospital.'

He frowned as if he wasn't sure that the idea was a good one any more.

'But of course we don't have a hospital in Spennymoor,' she went on. 'So it's up to us to look after the dying.'

7: WASTELAND

Tel's memory came back to him in bits and as each segment of nightmare vanished it was replaced with a fresh horror of the reality of the desolate park. It was the picture of Birdcage Walk that first jogged his mind, then the memory that he had been clutching a bottle of scotch, which the girl said she wished he still had. With her help, he talked himself back through the events in fits and starts until he remembered the pub and the meeting with his brother and he looked around to see where Bob had got to. From where they sat they could see the broken archway that led up the steps and into the street they had come down, but there was no sign of him. Finally, Tel realised that he was sitting next to the girl he had seen on the train.

'I never thought I'd get to talk to you,' he said. 'You looked so snotty.'

'And you looked too cocky by half.'

'I bet I didn't just now when you saw me coming over.'

She shook her head.

'How's your face?'

'It's funny. I hid under a car back there. I thought I'd be all right. But it feels all hot, burning.' Tel reached out to touch the soft skin round the red pulp but she shouted: 'Don't! That's what I did and the skin came off in my fingers.'

'Christ. We ought to get you to a doctor.'

The girl shrugged, 'Me and who else?' And her slim-fingered hands described the length and breadth of the park.

In the hour or so they had been sitting there, the place had been filling up. People were coming in mainly from the north, through Admiralty Arch and along the Mall, and, finding space, poured into it. After the violence of the falling buildings and the cauldron of the flames, the park seemed like an oasis, even though it was now no more than a patch of charred wasteland. They all came, tinker, tailor, rich man, poor man, some apparently unhurt, some with sores and swelling faces, some with skin that peeled off in sheets. The worst were near naked and so badly burned that little of their flesh remained pink. Some were running, some walking, some clinging to possessions: bags, cases, small bundles wrapped in cloth, an occasional crackling radio, even, for some reason, a portable typewriter. Most had nothing; their lives were evaporating and there was little to clutch. No help was at hand. The roads were impassable and, with fallout thick in the air and lumps of black rain pattering down, no one would would be in a hurry to search them out.

The worst injured remained in the park, unwilling or unable to carry on, but over all of them as they walked through the black, scrubby ground, there was a sorrow and an apathy that dragged at their feet. Whatever energy they had had had been expended in the initial escape from the broken buildings. Nor was there screaming or shouts, but a murmur, a buzz of moving sadness. None were in any doubt about the lethality of the explosion, and the inevitability of its effects seeped through them, weighing them down along with the real injuries. Those that kept moving were heading outwards, as they were all over London, following the perimeter of the spreading mushroom cloud which looked like nothing more than a grey day overhead. At the far end of the park, where only a few black fibres hung from the Buckingham Palace flagstaff where the Union Jack had proclaimed the Queen was in residence, they bottle-necked into the debris-strewn streets of Victoria. They wanted to get out, knowing death and an unimaginable hell was behind them. Yet they also knew they carried part of it with them, lurking in their blood and bones.

Neither Tel nor the girl had much idea about radioactivity or what atomic weapons did. They could see for themselves how it made people suffer and, from the complete blanket of smoke and huge red flames beyond Horse Guards Road to their right that told Tel it was unlikely he would see his family again, they could guess at the extent of the material damage. But to them, as to most people in the park, the strength and cause of the explosion was something unknown and they imagined a full-scale strike had reduced the city to ashes. And, for all they knew, wiped out half the western world as well. Either because of their ignorance or because of their feeling of insignificance, the two of them did not discuss it. What they did know, and what was of more immediate importance, was that they were in deep, deep trouble and that from now on they were on their own.

Across the lake in front of them a demolished cafe had already been plundered for cans of drink. The heat of the fires that were savaging the city and bursting in buildings all round the park was sucking the moisture from every pore. Those with throats so parched they thought they would die made for the lake and fell into the water, drinking, drinking. One or two did not come out again. Though Tel and the girl were thirsty, too, several passers-by had been warning people that the lake was poisoned. The radioactivity had not directly caused the deaths of the corpses in the water, but the sight of them was enough for the couple to believe they should stay away.

The girl offered Tel the last mint from a packet she had in her bag. 'What are we going to do?' she asked simply.

'I don't think the cavalry's going to turn up, that's for sure,' Tel stood up and looked around them. Any minute, he thought, Bob is going to appear with his cheery grin, telling us everything is all right, he's got something fixed. He had to find out what had happened to his brother, the last member of his family who might be left alive.

'Do you know it round here?' the girl asked.

'Not really.'

'Nor me. I'd just come up to see something at the ICA.' She looked towards the smoking buildings in the Mall. 'God, my mouth. It's so dry. It hurts to swallow.'

'But I do know there's a pub near here. Perhaps they'll have something to drink.' He hesitated, as if he was embarrassed, then he said: 'I know it sounds daft, but you haven't got a quid, have you? Just in case.'

The girl laughed and brought one out of her bag.

'Ta. Don't go away. *Please.*'

The look on his face said he meant it and she promised she would stay. As he ran off, back round the Leafpound, he really did hope she would be there when he got back. It might be a little while before he found out where his brother was, and hers was the only friendly face in the grotesque crowd.

If the park itself looked desolate, the buildings around it gave even less hope and as Tel ran beside the once proud bow-windowed Queen Anne buildings that had spilled their guts across the gardens beside Birdcage Walk he felt that, though his memory had returned, he might yet have died and crossed into another world. Small fires were puffing up smoke everywhere. The debris had filled up Cockpit Steps and Tel began climbing over it, setting his shoeless feet down carefully to get a grip and avoid the jagged edges. When he reached the top he imagined he would look down into Queen Anne's Gate and see the sign of the Two Chairmen hanging quietly among the dust, a haven in the ruins. There was nothing of the sort. Yellow bricks, lime mortar, lath and plaster which hadn't seen the light of day for more than two hundred years lay strewn in a succession of heaps under which, Tel shivered to think, Bob would surely be. For if he had two legs to walk on he would have gone into the park and found Tel sitting there. Almost running across the humps, the dips, the plateaux, catching his falls with his outstretched hands, he called his brother's name. But the reply he got was not what he expected. A dozen voices came back from beneath the mess, all from different directions, all calling out for help. 'Bob?' he yelled sharply and again there was a clamour for help, mixed with the moans of pain and despair.

The Two Chairmen had stood, he reckoned, about fifty yards back from Cockpit Steps and the hump and dip of the rubble and the piles of roof slates mapped out the street. When he reached what he thought was the spot, he called out again. This time the response came from several voices from somewhere beneath his feet. With his hands he began a task he knew would be a challenge to a mechanical digger. Bit by bit the debris was pulled aside and every now and then he would say his brother's name. Still nobody called back: 'Tel!'

When a man in a torn shirt, with small, bloody nicks on his cheeks, came by, Tel asked him to lend a hand. 'My brother's in there,' he said. 'There's others, too.'

'I've been looking all the time,' the man said distantly. 'I can't find anyone I know.' Nevertheless he climbed down beside him and they set to work.

'Bloody politicians,' he said after a while. 'If they could see what it's like over there.' He nodded towards the underground. 'It's every disaster you ever thought of, all piled up together. There's a dead baby . . .' His voice trailed off, then he said: 'I was going to the park to see if I could get some water.'

'There's nothing there. It's all poisoned. When are they going to start bringing some help, anyway?'

'They? Who's they? You won't get anybody coming out in this weather. They'll come looking for us when we're dead.'

It was only confirmation. Tel already realised it was time everyone helped themselves. After about half an hour, when they had dug down a few feet, the man said it really was time he found some water, but he promised to be back. Tel didn't bother to watch him lumber off towards the park. He knew he would not see him again.

It was getting dark when the first casualty came to light. Trapped beneath a beam, first an arm, then his chest and head appeared. Though his face was pinched and white, there didn't seem to be any other injury apart from the crushed legs. Discovering the man could talk, Tel was describing his brother to him when a loud explosion took his breath away. Burning wood crackled nearby and they both felt the heat.

'Get me out of here, for God's sake.'

'But did you see him?' Tel shouted desperately.

'Yes, yes, the joker,' the man said. 'He left that behind.' He flicked his head towards the black cavern behind him. Tel peered into the darkness and could not even tell if it was the inside or the outside of the building. 'The briefcase.'

'Didn't he come back for it?'

'No.' He was looking over Tel's shoulder towards the flames. 'We never saw him again.'

'So that evening, they go to all the nightspots: Talk of the Town, Raymond's Revue Bar . . . two, three o'clock in the morning. And the two of them get paralytic . . .'

'Just like you. Leave the jokes out, will you?' Jeffrey chucked another brick towards the darkness and the sound of scurrying paws.

Bob leaned back on the bricks and closed his eyes. 'Rats,' he sighed.

'How many of these beasts are there?' Jeffrey asked.

'In Britain they outnumber people three or four times,' John told him, stroking his beard. 'The problem is, with the sewage system broken down, they're going to get very hungry soon. Then they'll all start to come out, not just in here but up on the ground, too. Some of them are quite resistant to radiation.'

Beat coughed. 'Talking of food, my tummy's rumbling.'

'Is it?' John sounded surprised, as if she was complaining of a between-meal hunger gap. He opened up his briefcase. 'Well, there are a few bits and pieces here. Biscuits, milk ...'

'Now he tells us,' said Jeffrey. 'What else have you got in there?'

'Not much. Some aspirin.'

Bob's eyes popped open. 'Oh goody, drugs. Can I have some, please? My hangover's already coming on.'

John shook some into his hand and when he asked if anyone else wanted any, they all said they did. None of them was feeling well. The nauseous fumes were already well-established inside them and although it was only early evening, the events of the day, combined with the long, empty hours of sitting around, helped to bring on fatigue. Each of them had found a place to sit among the bricks some distance from where the leg had appeared. Jeffrey, however, could not sit still. He had been pacing up and down, keeping guard on the rats and firing questions off at John about nuclear weapons, radiation and what they could expect to see outside. John's answers had been short and to the point. He didn't revel in his knowledge or pass any judgement or blame. Nor did he dwell on the horrors of the bomb's effects.

Eating a biscuit now, with a hand cupped beneath his chin to prevent rat-attracting crumbs from falling, Jeffrey said: 'I think I actually might give my right arm to be out of here.'

Alan looked up with a tight smile. He couldn't resist it. 'Give it to me and I'll let you go.'

'Oh, piss off, Mr Smartass Greengrass.'

It wasn't just the sudden rudeness that made Alan look startled. He had told nobody about his plan to unseat Bishop, let alone the name he had put on the file he had kept locked inside his desk. It all seemed so petty now, so long ago, and he laughed nervously. Despite the venom he had felt towards his fellow director in the past few days, a reminder of it at this moment was merely an embarrassment.

But Jeffrey wouldn't let it drop. 'What do you think I am? Some kind of business studies graduate still wet behind the ears? Jesus, you were lucky today. You would have come out of that meeting with egg all over your face. And none of the directors, not even the nice Miss Beatrix Simmons here, would have felt like offering you a hanky to wipe it off.'

'What are you talking about?' Alan was unsure. He did not know if Bishop had discovered the file in the wastepaper bin on the way out of Beat's office, or if he really knew about it. Nor did he know whether to quell his reawakening spleen: it was just possible Bishop was cracking, putting all his frustrations of the disaster back into an older battle whose rules he understood.

'Your private life's a mess,' Jeffrey muttered.

'Huh! The lounge lizard in a dog collar. It doesn't fit, not someone like you who'd stick it in a light socket just to boost your ego.'

It was too late. He had said it. He glanced at Beat but she was already looking the other way. Bob had begun to whistle 'Nellie Dean'.

'Well at least my wife doesn't sleep around, and if she did she'd know better than to bunk up with a hatchet man who's trying to put us all out of business.'

Alan had had enough. Of the stinking sewer, of his hands that would not stop stinging, of the present company and of his private life. Yes, it was a mess. 'Where did you say the tunnel was?'

'What?'

'The tunnel. You said you saw one just now, like the one we came down.'

'About fifty yards back on the right.'

'Right, then. Outside.'

'Oh, for crying out loud,' said Beat. 'If men behave like you two, it's not surprising we've all ended up like this.'

Jeffrey ignored her. 'Outside,' he agreed.

But they never made it. John suddenly called them to hush and because they had grown used to listening to what he said, the squabble stopped. His eyes were peering forward in the darkness and it was not difficult to imagine his ears pricked like a dog's. It was a moment before the others heard it. A splashing sound, a pounding, the noise of running feet. A few minutes later there was the breath, hot from exertion, panting with the rhythm of the strides. Finally the figure, naked but for tattered underpants, the head quite bald, the face swelling and marked with purple patches, a flap of skin hanging from his left arm. It was impossible to tell how old he was. The candlelight fell on him before he knew they were there.

'Sorry.' His voice was surprisingly strong and he spoke as if he'd pushed open the wrong door in a hotel. 'Sorry, I, er ...' The index finger of his right hand went up in the air and shook a little, trying to help him think. 'It's the bloody keys. Can't find them anywhere. The wife's out and she'd have a fit if I tried to break a window. They're around somewhere. Small bunch. Got a medallion on them. St Christopher.' Refusing to meet their gazes, his eyes roamed the floor, searching for what he had lost. Suddenly he began to cry uncontrollably. None of the others went to help, nor could they think of anything to say. The sight of him, the tragedy of his face, kept them where they were. 'They're only a bunch of keys, I know. But I need them. Can't get home without them. Car keys are on it, too ...'

He turned away and they saw that there was no skin on his back and what remained was raw, red and pulsating. Alan gagged and the others turned their heads away, taking with them the particular image that would haunt most of them as long as they lived. But Jeffrey could not take his eyes from the apparition that was disappearing into the darkness it had come from, weeping.

Jeffrey turned and looked at the others. Bob's eyes were closed. Alan and John were looking at the floor and Beat was quietly crying. He turned away again and followed the man down the tunnel, not walking quickly enough to catch him up. Nobody asked him where he was going but it was a good guess that he would be heading for the pipe he and Alan had thought of climbing through to continue their personal war. There was no attempt to stop him.

Twenty minutes later, when one of the two candles stuck

on to the bricks beside them began to gutter, Alan broke the silence. 'Oh, no,' he said tiredly. 'He's gone off with all the candles.'

The face that Tel would never forget belonged to the man trapped beneath the beam beside the Two Chairmen. Not because he felt any particular sympathy for him, nor because his injuries were especially hideous. But because he had left him there to die. Whatever had sparked off the explosion – a gas pipe, perhaps – kept the flames well fed while the two of them struggled to shift the lump of timber. Eventually Tel had said he was going to fetch help, knowing, just as it had been with the man from the underground, that he would not return. There was no way he could have announced: 'You've had it, mate. I'm off.' Yet that is what they both knew he was saying.

The explosion had blown a hole between them and the park and the flames from it were streaming twenty feet into the air. To avoid them, Tel had to return by a circuitous route across the brittle heaps of former buildings from which cries for help still came. When he reached the park, by skidding down into the garden of one of the listed houses governments had agreed should be maintained for posterity, and clambering over the paint-stripped railings, he stood in the darkening evening for a full five minutes watching the fire. He saw Bob in it, chuckling, living, a phoenix in a funeral pyre.

The reverie was abruptly halted by a single shot. Two hundred yards to his right Rosamund lay still beside the cars, the policeman kneeling by her head. Dry-eyed and his mind a vacuum from which deeper feelings were sucked, Tel walked back into the park to find his only friend on earth. On the path a charred, flat square of wood was in the way and though his socks were torn and his feet were scratched, he kicked it. It skidded across the tarmac, leaving behind a sheet of paper, untouched. Out of curiosity he flipped it over and was surprised to see a map of St James's and The Green Park. He studied the outlined shapes, not knowing what he was looking for until he found it – a grey segment on the far left, overprinted with the words 'St George's Hospital'. Now he had somewhere to go and suddenly he knew how to get there. Despite his tiredness, the twin revelations gave his feet new energy and he ran to find the girl.

She was not where he had left her. You promised, you promised, his head shouted and he looked round wildly. In fact she wasn't far away but she was no longer alone. Two lads their own age were with her. He went over and said hello and they returned the greeting. There was dirt on their hands and faces, a few small cuts, and their clothes were torn. The ironic message on the white lad's T-shirt was still visible beneath the grime: 'Free the London seven million'.

'Did you get anything?' the girl asked. She looked more tired now and in the dusk the patch on her cheek seemed black.

'Fraid not.' His throat was swollen from the heat and exertion and he would have loved a drink himself. 'But I found a hospital and I got us some transport, too.'

'Any room for us?' one of the boys wanted to know.

'Why not? If you can give us a hand hooking up the trailer.'

Tel put a hand on the girl's shoulder and guided her towards the Leafpound, the others walking one on each side. Again he apologised for not finding any drink.

'Never mind, it's a bit better now,' she said. 'Marvin here had a good idea. We had a drink from the radiator of one of those cars. He used a biro like a straw. It was pretty awful. We couldn't really drink it, so we just washed our mouths out.'

'I swallowed half of it and it was diabolical.' Marvin looked as if he had come from Trinidad but he sounded as if he lived down Tel's road. 'But at least it shouldn't have been contaminated.'

'You'll probably die of Radseal poisoning,' the one in the T-shirt said.

'Marvin said there's only been one bomb,' said the girl.

'Someone told me he heard it on the radio,' he confirmed. 'It was an accident. Probably one of those nuclear trains that go through London. The authorities want us to stay where we are, not go anywhere.'

'Stuff that,' said Tel.

They had reached the Leafpound where the tractor Tel had seen a few hours earlier stood like a contender for the breaker's yard. But the damage was mainly to the paintwork and the glass around the cab. Though he knew they could have started the diesel engine with a hefty shove, Tel was glad to see the keys were still in the ignition. When they had hitched up one of the mesh-box trailers, the others climbed aboard and the girl rested her head against a pillow made out of Marvin's jacket. Tired grey rings were growing round her eyes. Inside the cab, Tel straddled the driving seat and tried to figure out how the levers and instruments worked. It caught first go and when he tugged at the hand throttle it gave an optimistic roar, a strange sound of life and recovery that startled the park. Tel felt like a racing driver on the grid. He found the lights, slipped the clutch and they were off.

The wind didn't actually streak through Tel's hair as he negotiated the Leafpound and made his way back up to the lake, but the whiff of moving air under his nostrils was cooling enough and he felt at last something was happening. The tractor lined up to cross the narrow bridge that spanned the lake but halfway over it the lights picked out a metal barrier, twisted and broken at the far end. When Tel touched the far right-hand pedal, the vehicle slewed to the right and immediately he realised why there were two pedals beneath his right foot. He kicked the other one and they lurched to the left and came to a stop.

'What's going on?' Tommy shouted.

'There's a barrier up there.'

'Well, knock it down.'

Tel revved the engine and accelerated towards the bars. There was a bump and a scream of metal and the girl was thrown on to her side. But they were through, heading for The Mall. All around them people were gathering like black crows lurking in the gloom. The full beams turned their heads and picked out their distress, their wounds, their chill panic and their trudging despair. In the slow process of escape this was a lifeboat ploughing through a sea of survivors and by the time it reached the gate leading into The Mall, it had begun filling up. They climbed aboard, some with shouts, most in silence, hauling themselves up inside the craft and clawing with desperate fingers to the outside of the cage. An ageing American woman who had lost half her silver hair was pushed aboard by her husband who tripped and fell before the helping hands could reach him. With one lens in his glasses missing, the other cracked, he did not see the camera looped around his neck being crunched beneath a tractor wheel. Shouts from the passengers brought the tractor to a stop and he was hauled up to join them.

The Mall was as hopelessly blocked as Birdcage Walk had been and Tel swung the tractor to the left between the speckled sticks of remnant plane trees, the wheels chasing pedestrians and flattening the charred carcasses of fallen pigeons. Desperately he peered along the six lanes of cars, looking for a gap that would take them through to the other side where they could head onwards towards Green Park and the hospital. Ahead of them, beyond the blocked circus of Queen's Gardens, Buckingham Palace stood solidly sombre, some of its broken windows issuing smoke, and its dull facade warmed by the yellowing reflection of the fires that were burning in the city and that had flared up all around. By the time they had reached the jam around the fallen statue of the Victoria memorial, it was clear there was no getting through. Tel switched off the engine and jumped down from the cab, leaving the lights beaming whitely.

'It's no good,' he announced to his passengers. 'We can't go any further.'

They began to disembark, none with thanks, some with a single look that told him he had let them down. The two boys helped the girl to the ground. They were glad to get out of there. The proximity of their travelling companions, the boxed crush of the injured with their moans and stories of how they had got this far, of what they had left behind, weighed badly on all of them. Tel took the girl's hand.

'Which way?' Marvin asked.

Tel pointed to the far side of the Palace. 'Up round there, at the end of the next bit of park.'

'What, Knightsbridge?'

'Dunno.'

'Come on, Den.'

Marvin slapped his friend on the shoulder and the two were off across the pressed-steel pack, pounding on bonnets, roofs and boots to get to the other side. As the girl watched them go Tel squeezed her hand and said: 'You're cold.' Then he steered her between the cars. In the light from the unquenchable fire they could easily make out their shapes, and just as easily see the occupants who had been left behind in the tyranny of shattered glass. By one of them Tel stopped and opened the driver's door. The body had fallen forwards and it was only when Tel pulled it back that the fatal lacerations showed.

'What are you doing?' the girl asked.

'Getting you a coat.' He had begun easing the sheepskin off the stiff shoulders.

'I don't need it. Leave him alone.'

Tel shrugged and let the body go. 'Down to you,' he said, and they carried on across the memorial's steps before squeezing themselves again between the cars. At the far side, where Constitution Hill took the road up past the Palace to Belgravia, the white lights of a car came on and an engine started up, followed by the sound of a succession of crashes, metal against metal. When they reached Green Park, they saw a Mercedes pull out from the ranks, its front crunched up by the battering it had taken when it had pushed away the cars to give it space to get out. It lurched towards them, then slid to a squealing halt. A rear door flew open and Marvin called: 'Get in.'

It was luxury to slump into the cloth seats and the feel of them about their worn bodies made them think of sleep.

'Tasty motor, isn't it?' Dennis was at the wheel. 'Always wanted to drive one of these.'

In the front the two boys kept their heads close to where the windscreen had been, peering at the figures that popped into the spotlight. If St James's had been filling with people, this wasteland was teeming and it was a slow and bumpy ride across the once green park. But this time no one tried to climb aboard, though some peered in to see who had been chosen to ride in the limousine.

They got as far as Wellington Place, opposite the hospital, when they were forced to stop. Staring ahead to see what was in their way, Tel and the girl saw a dozen officers of the law collecting like moths around the headlights. They were no credit to the force: their uniforms were dirty and they looked as tired as anyone in the parks. Among them were several men in civilian clothes which could not hide their vocation, and in the hands of some of them were small guns. At least, Tel thought, they would let them cross the road to reach their goal.

The engine faded and a uniformed policeman walked towards them as if he were pulling them up for a speeding offence. He bent down and shone a torch inside the window, first in the front, then in the back, going over their faces carefully. The girl shivered.

Keeping the torch beam on the driver, he said: 'All transport has been requisitioned. No vehicles can be driven without express authority.'

'We were just trying to get this lady to a hospital,' Tel said and the light flicked round to him.

'What hospital?'

'St George's. Over there.'

'Well, if it was open, there'd be quite a queue by now. As it is, they closed the place down years ago.'

8: NEWS

An army helicopter had come and gone, droning in from the east, its blades thudding above the town. It brought no news, no supplies. It might have been from another country, another planet. After watching the activity of the roundabout, of the movements around the roads and buildings, it seemed to become bored and it drifted off to the west.

The communications breakdown was caused by four separate effects of the explosion. The first was the electromagnetic pulse given off by the light flash which had temporarily upset airwaves in all but the remotest parts of the country. The second was that this pulse, fed into aerials, had blown transistors in radios, televisions, receivers and walkie-talkies. Some silicon chips and printed circuits had also fried. The third was from the power surge through the mains supply which overloaded systems causing extensive damage, not least to transmission stations. The fourth was damage to communication towers which had been twisted or bent or, nearer the blast, completely destroyed. Two hours after the explosions the police in Spennymoor, with the help of a Post Office engineer, were still attempting to repair their radio equipment when the first news came into the town, not from the police or army, but from a white commercial van that hurtled towards the roundabout from the south, nipping a few millimetres of tread from its tyres as it screamed to a stop by the congested road block. The young driver jumped from the vehicle and grinned at the arm-banded policeman who was immediately by his side.

'Medical supplies.' He jabbed his thumb over his shoulder and announced the names of the proprietary drugs. 'We weren't quite sure what was happening to you up here but we thought I might as well come, in case you needed them. The traffic's diabolical. There's all kinds of problems.' He couldn't keep still. He was jumping about on his toes.

'Just a minute, just a minute. Who's "we"?'

'Breakers. CB radio. I was down near Darlington when the

bomb went off, out of the worst of it. But it blew away a lot of rigs ...'

The policeman peered into the van and saw the radio gear that cluttered the dashboard. By the sheer amount of it, it was undoubtedly illegal. 'Is it working now?'

'Affirmative. You want to talk to the anchor man? He's got a big bear with him.'

'Talk English, you daft bugger.'

When the driver explained that he was in touch with an operator in Darlington where a police sergeant was standing by, the official went to fetch the inspector. Climbing into the passenger seat he cautiously took the mike and depressed the push-to-talk bar as he was shown. The relief of talking to somebody on the outside showed on his heavy face and when he introduced himself he smiled tightly as if they were face to face. Four bombs had gone off: one up there in Durham, one in Aberdeen, one in London and one off the coast of Lincolnshire and Norfolk, in The Wash. They were looking into the causes and the military was still on red alert. Police and army rescue parties were already out concentrating on clearing the motorway but there were numerous accidents and breakdowns which had to be cleared. People were evacuated down the east coast, from Seaham, Easington and Peterlee. In the hospitals all over the country, any patient who could walk was being sent home but in Newton Aycliffe, Darlington, Middlesbrough and Hartlepool they were already full. The co-ordinated effort now was aimed at boxing in the area by controlling the A68, the old Roman road about ten miles to the west that ran straight as could be from just outside Bishop Auckland, up to Consett, through the Tyne Valley, the Cheviot Hills and on to Edinburgh. That and the North Sea would form the two sides while the bottom of the box would be the A689 from Bishop Auckland to Hartlepool. By commanding these roads they could contain traffic movement and stop people 'roaming about'. Finally, the inspector asked when they might expect help, giving an estimate of the casualties who had arrived and a list of the things that they needed. There was a pause when he let go of the push-to-talk bar and for a moment he thought he had lost contact.

'We have a Roentgen count of 200 for you.' The inspector confirmed it. 'The "stay put" orders are still operating and we've been told not to take risks but some army people should be up with you soon. We're just waiting to see which way the wind blows.' When the inspector didn't reply, he went on: 'Have you got trouble up there?'

'You're not kidding.'

'Well, I'll see what we can do, but I can't promise anything.'

They signed off. To get through to the outside world after all this and be told that there could be no promise of help was a heavy blow. His face was pale and he looked rather sick.

'We'll get you some stuff, chief,' the young driver said, to cheer him up. 'Just name it. There are lorries pulled in by the road all over the country, carrying anything anybody could want – bread, milk, meat, clothes, hospital equipment. There's even a prefabricated nuclear shelter on its way to Carlisle ...'

About a mile away, in a garden shed behind a rather bizarrely baroque Victorian house in the southern end of the town, news was coming in from a second source. A Post Office employee was leaning over a radio ham who had picked up a fellow enthusiast on the other side of the Pennines, in Preston. When the alarm had been raised he had disconnected the electricity supply from the set and afterwards wired it to a car battery, fixed up a voltage amplifier and had now got it working again. The very low frequency it used was unaffected by the flash and blast. There were no worries now about using the equipment outside the licence's brief of talking only about radio problems and 'educational' matters, and the voice on the other end rapidly spelled out what was going on. News in Lancashire was being broadcast by the local radio and the main concern was still that people should stay indoors. Messages about local congestion made up the bulk of the information but from contacts with other hams round the country a broader picture had emerged. With the first warning, everything that could fly seemed to have taken off and though some RAF and USAF aircraft were beginning to return to their bases, there was still a high volume of activity on the airwaves, particularly around military airports and bases. The army was on the move all over the country and roads were forbidden to all but official traffic. After sunset tonight there would also be a curfew and only civilians in stricken areas would be allowed on the streets. Great Britain had been divided into three. Scotland was to take care of Aberdeen. With Newcastle now in no position to organise the north-east, the task had been handed on to the UK Land Forces Headquarters in York, who would work together with the Headquarters of the north-west section operating from Preston. The rest of the country would take care of London and the evacuation of populations round The Wash where there had been some indirect casualties. There was little chance of rescuing those on the remaining rigs in the North Sea gas fields now in flames and boiling the sea for miles around. An earlier report that two American planes had been shot down by Soviet fighters over Finland had not been confirmed.

At the police station in Spennymoor these two reports were collated and the Roentgen count was taken again. The inspector, arriving after delivering the van to the health centre, took the information to the district council, where a map of Britain was pinned to the wall. Though the information he had was not of immediate importance to many of the people in the town, it was of more than passing concern and those who could stopped to listen and look at the map, trying to imagine the scale of the damage across the country. It was reasonable to suppose that Newcastle, though not directly hit, would nevertheless be in a disastrous position, with no water, electricity or gas supplies. Nobody could tell if it would also be affected by radiation but with winds seeming to be settling down to south-south-west, it was likely. It was also likely that the fallout would be drifting across to Sunderland and the mouth of the Wear.

'I wonder if they'll use that bunker under the Civic Centre they keep going on about.'

'They'll be eaten alive if they ever get out of there.'

'It certainly won't improve their chances at the next election.'

From beyond the room a woman suddenly called the chief executive's name and the group all turned towards the door.

Coming through it were three men, two of them armed with heavy automatic weapons, all of them in khaki gloves and suits and masks which covered their heads. They looked like mutants, humanoid ants from a science-fiction film.

The unarmed one looked around him and stepped forward making no attempt to remove his mask. 'Is this the War Council?' His voice was raised but it sounded distant, as if it were coming from the bottom of a mine shaft.

'It's the district council,' the chief executive said. 'Who are you?'

He introduced himself, a lieutenant from a unit which had been dispatched from York. He looked around him, the mutant head twitching as it studied the groups, then turned back to the chief executive. 'I'd like a word ...'

'It's all right, laddie, we're all in the same boat.'

The mutant head was still for a moment, then it nodded. 'We're just a reconnaissance unit. We're setting up a field hospital in the grounds of the Bishop's palace in Auckland. That's where you should send your sick. The road will be kept clear as far as we can from our end but there's to be no evacuation. It's just for the casualties or emergencies. Our resources are already overstretched and you should only send those people who look as if they have a reasonable chance of recovery.'

'There's nobody in this town,' said Maggie, swinging into her argument again, 'who could tell you who is going to live or die. We're not washing our hands of anybody.'

The pressing together of his two gloved hands was a sign of the officer's embarrassment. 'I understand,' he said. 'But it might not be in their best interests. The field hospital will only be accepting those they think will live.'

The hatred in Maggie's eyes was there to be seen and she made no attempt to conceal it.

'In the meantime,' the officer went on quickly, 'we have brought a signals unit with us to keep you in touch with the HQ at York. You're under their jurisdiction now, of course.'

'Of course,' the chief executive echoed. 'What was it that went off? Can we expect any more bombs?'

'I don't know. Britain has been hit by five warheads.' He turned his head towards their map where four red circles had been drawn. 'Just about as you have it there, except that there have been two here, not one. One went off up by a place called Pity Me on the north side of Durham City, the other one was six miles past that in Chester-le-Street.' If the hush of his audience took a different tone as the new knowledge enlarged the picture of the horror that had been brought, the officer didn't notice it, and he went on: 'Each weapon is of the same type and strength, 200 kilotons, and they were all ground bursts.'

'Soviet missiles?'

'No. Nobody knows why yet, but they came from three missiles launched from a submarine on a routine exercise off the coast of Greenland. It was one of our own Polaris submarines, *Resolution*.'

This time the shock of the audience was audible and the comments not entirely polite.

'This information has not yet been broadcast as they are still looking into it. But the reason I have been instructed to tell you is because there's something else. Each Polaris missile has three warheads but only the missile itself is targeted ...'

'On us?'

'... and when the warheads break away from the missile, they just scatter by themselves, willy-nilly, usually in an area of about ten square miles. They're pretty inaccurate sort of things. We're fairly sure that the two others that did not detonate in Aberdeen fell into the sea. For some reason the one in the south broke up early and scattered further than usual, with one landing in The Wash, the other on London. We've found the third one near Cambridge. But here only two have exploded, so that leaves a third one unexploded somewhere between here and Newcastle. If anybody sees anything that looks like a missile, get in touch with us at once on that radio we've brought. And for goodness sake, don't touch it.'

The thought that anyone might be fool enough to do so brought laughter that came more as a release of nerves than from any sense of amusement. There were questions, of course, but as soon as he could, the chief executive got down to talking to the lieutenant about more specific matters closer to hand. They were joined by the inspector and together they pored over the local map, looking at the roads and searching for areas where help or hindrance might come from.

While they talked a constable came into the room. He stopped nervously short when he saw the armed men, then, catching the inspector's eye nodded agitatedly towards the door. The inspector excused himself and followed the constable from the room.

'Sorry to trouble you, sir,' he whispered when they were out of earshot. 'It's the police from Darlington. They say they've heard we've got trouble.'

'I should hope they have.'

'But two bloody great meat wagons have just arrived. They've got riot shields in them. And helmets. And cannisters of CS gas ...'

Those who came in from Durham, by foot, by bike, by car, by any means they could, brought with them stories of a city which did not have long to live. As far as it was possible to tell, there had been no firestorm, but the damaged and flattened buildings were nevertheless now being consumed in flames. A second road block, up near Mount Pleasant, ensured that all refugees coming into town were directed either to the health centre or to the queue of people waiting to be taken to Bishop Auckland, further south. Many of the arrivals were from the university, from the nearest colleges of Neville's Cross, Trevellyan and St Mary's and each one brought an appeal for help for those they had left behind. There was none to be had. Angry, sickened and with a sense of betrayal, some had turned round and gone back into the town and the radiation, knowing the risks they were running, to return again later with more casualties.

When Dr MacGilvray had told the inspector not to leave anybody out in the open, he had not entirely realised just how many would arrive. As the night began to draw in on the day nobody ever wanted to see again, there must have been nearly a thousand in the town and two or three times that number had gone on elsewhere. Yet the term-time population of Durham was nearly 30,000 and, perversely, he had to hope there would still be thousands more to come. Within half an hour of his arriving, the health centre had burst its seams and casualties spilled over into the sports centre a hundred yards away, where patients were stretched out in a chaos of untidy rows. Social workers, WRVS, anybody in the town with a minimum medical knowledge had come to help while the education authorities supplied food from the school canteens. The doctor had long ago given up any idea of treating anybody, assigning to himself the role of initial diagnosis and drug distribution. Patching up was done by the young doctor, by a GP who had managed to get away from his surgery and nurses from the training college in Bishop Auckland who lived in Spennymoor. Though there was no cure for the radiation sickness, there were medicines to alleviate some of the worst cases of vomiting and diarrhoea. There was blindness and retinal burns from the flash, burst eardrums and haemorrhaging from the blast and numerous cuts, wounds and fractures from the falling glass and buildings. And there were the terrible burns which left flesh hanging off like stripped wallpaper. These were the hardest to deal with, the cases which apparently no hospital in the country would now touch. Among all these wounds the doctor could detect other symptoms, too, ones that they had neither the facilities nor the time to attend. Bandages were being peeled off by the yard, antiseptic solutions made up by the bucketful, empty tubes of antiseptic cream overflowed from bins. It would be a miracle if no diseases ran riot through such a place and he was constantly reminding everyone to keep everything clean. To compound the suffering, night was coming on and although generators had been set up to provide light, it was going to get terribly cold.

When he next returned to the health centre there was a welcome sight for him, an old green municipal water lorry from Newton Aycliffe was drawing up outside. Without exception those who had been brought in for treatment were all suffering from some sort of dehydration and liquids were fast running out. They could do with all the water they could drink. A student who had just arrived with two companions called out if he could have a drop and the driver told him to wait. Inside the building Maggie was looking for MacGilvray and when he came through the doors she took him to one side to tell him of the army's arrival. Despite their edict that all help stopped at Bishop Auckland she would ask them to try to get anything the doctor might want.

'Just three things,' he said drily. 'Morphine, morphine and morphine.'

Maggie sighed. 'Anything else?'

'Bandages. Calcium and vitamin tablets, tranquillisers, syringes – I've already caught someone using a needle twice. And I don't suppose there's any chance of it but I'd be grateful if you put in a plea again for a blood transfusion unit.'

She promised to try her best and the doctor turned to go into the surgery. This time he was trapped by a woman in her forties. Short and skinny, she looked as if she had probably not had three square meals a day all her life, yet among the casualties she was a picture of health. With her were three other women, all in outdoor coats. When she spoke, it was in the manner of somebody unused to talking to those in authority.

'What is it?' MacGilvray asked, rather too sharply.

'We're from over on the estate. None of us have had any medical training, but we've all had families, children to look after. We have a dozen beds between us. They say they're only looking after the patients who are likely to live and we thought that the others ... well, we could at least try to make them comfortable. If you would just tell us what to do.'

The doctor looked at them for a moment, wondering if they really knew what they were taking on. There was no doubt that they were resolute.

'That's a welcome idea, ladies,' he said in the end. 'You stay here and I'll find you some patients. Let me just have a word with the doctor in here first.'

Before he reached the door he heard a commotion outside. The water lorry had started up and was pulling away down the road. The driver was shouting after it. The doctor looked over towards the students by the door. There were only two of them there now and without being told he knew that the other one would be trying to take the lorry out of the town and into Durham. It was a blow to have lost such a valuable vehicle but as he listened to it disappearing up the road to Mount Pleasant and the road block, he couldn't help wishing the young man luck.

9: NIGHT

'What on earth possessed me to ask Bishop to step outside? I can't imagine ... I can't imagine anything any more. If what John says is right, millions are dead out there. *Millions.* How can anyone understand that; I can't even begin to conceive of it ... nothing adds up. One thought just won't go alongside another any more. I simply can't grasp what it is we're actually meant to be doing down here. Just how *are* we supposed to behave when something so devastating is going on? It's made the whole process of thinking completely obsolete. There isn't even any reason to plan what we might do when we get out of here tomorrow because the chances are there won't be anything left up there. Nothing.'

'The insurance claims should keep us busy for a while.'

Alan could see no point in making a joke, though he was glad Beat was still sitting with him. She could not know that, as he spoke, he was gently rocking backwards and forwards, his hands pressed together, pushing against the growing pain of the cuts in his palms. The luminous digits on his watch had told him it was past midnight and the snoring on his right made him jealous that Bob, by some miracle not unconnected with best part of a bottle of Sçotch, had found it possible to float away into sleep. About ten minutes earlier John had got up from his seat on the bricks in the fallen rubble and gone off back down the sewer. In the lighter's firefly glow that came and went in the distance, he was looking for alternative ways they could escape when the worst of the fall-out had gone. The others, he had said, should stay where they were and, with the thought that anyone else like the man in search of his keys might still be in the tunnel, they had taken little persuading. Alan was left with just half a box of matches which he did not dare use for fear of expending them too fast. Disorientated in the dark, he had been talking on for some while, unimpeded, his tired voice a small but important comfort in the darkness.

'Poor John,' he went on, 'I feel sorry for him, trying to get to his wife and children. He's a good chap to have around, we were lucky. Maybe he's lucky, too, having a goal, a home to get to must help keep him going through all this. Bishop was right, my life is a mess – was a mess. It's rather fitting that I should end up in here along with the excrement. There's nothing up there that I'm proud of, nothing I can look to and say I've left that behind. There was somebody in the hotel this morning who wanted to borrow a shaving brush and when I offered him mine he took one look at it and said he'd go out and buy one. God, was it only this morning?'

Beat didn't respond, stubbornly and uncharacteristically refusing to help someone out of the doldrums.

If she wasn't going to listen, then Alan would not care what he said. He pushed on: 'When I saw you two in your office, I was so completely thrown, I didn't know what to think. I really loathed you at first, both of you, but now it seems a bit silly to hate anything. There's nowhere left for feelings to go; all the guns have been spiked.' Again he paused and again Beat refused to be drawn. 'Do you know, when I left, I passed by Mead's office and Miss Nielson was still in there typing out correspondence for him. I told her to come down to the basement but she wouldn't. She was going to spend her last minutes on earth typing letters that would never get posted.'

At last Beat intervened, coming not to the defence of Alan or Bishop or even herself but of someone who wasn't able to speak for themself. 'She was one of the people who kept that place going,' she said. 'The milk that makes the people at the top think they're the cream. She's been with the company years, working conscientiously, and perhaps if she had broken the pattern, even at a time like this – or especially at a time like this – she would have felt lost.'

'I should have stayed up there, too,' Alan said feebly. 'I wonder how Bishop's made out. Did he really know about Greengrass?'

'What's Greengrass?' In her tiredness, the question was automatic.

'The end of the sales manager. I dropped it in the wastepaper basket when I left your office. It was a dossier I'd got together of evidence of Bishop's backhanders. Everything was all true, authenticated, it took me a long time. He couldn't have wriggled out of it, whatever he said earlier on.'

'Really?' A note of interest showed a more familiar Beat, enthusiastic, keen for news, and Alan immediately recalled the brown eyes, wide with flattering attentiveness that could bring out the best in people. 'Tell me about it.'

So he told the story, detail by detail, clue by clue, with as much, if not more satisfaction than he would have had at the meeting earlier that day, building it up to the grand slam, the final exorcism.

When he had finished, Beat said: 'That's brilliant, Alan, you got him at last.'

'What are you talking about?'

'What?'

'But you were screwing him up there. On the floor of your office ...'

She sniffed. 'I panicked.'

'Oh, come on, I know you better than that. You don't panic, you're always in control. I mean I know I've got no rights on your body ...'

'Quite.'

'... but Jeffrey Bishop. If it had been the office messenger I wouldn't have minded half so much.'

There was a silence in which Alan held his defiance and when Beat began to speak it was in the even tones of suppressed anger.

'Look, Alan, you don't have a right to know and in no way do I owe you an explanation but if you're looking for a bit of truth, I'll give you some. Let's get it straight: you and a dozen others I could mention at Pennines – including Jeffrey, yes – you use me like some fucking agony aunt up there. You disappear for weeks, then something happens to you, something that's upset you or something you want to crow about, and you trot along to see me. Okay, I like gossip, I'm actually interested in what's going on, not just with the company but with the people who make it. People's lives are, after all, about a million times more interesting than any file says – or they should be or I've got it all wrong. Did you know, for instance, that Jeffrey's father is actually illiterate?' Alan didn't. 'Now that's something that interests me about him. I'm not talking about any pulling-himself-up-by-the-bootstraps cliché, nor am I saying that he's an Eistedfodd poetry candidate. That isn't the point. It just helps us to know, to get on with each other. So what I'm saying is, yes, I like to hear about everyone and what's going on, but you all just take from me all the time. And then, and then when I do something out of the ordinary – extraordinary for you because you haven't been thinking about *me* – you resort to cheap talk about the office messenger.'

Punctured, Alan was silent, looking at himself with Beat's guidance. It was true what she said and he couldn't protest. The last time he had spoken more than a few words to her was a week or two back when he had taken her to lunch and got the conversation round to telling her that he and Madeleine had broken up. Of all people, he had known that she would listen best, a good ear, a good egg, who knew about bad patches and downers. But what had she told him about herself at that meal? What had he asked her? The fact that he could not remember proved her case.

'On the other hand, among them all, you're the best, though I'm not quite sure how good that is.' It was the consolation prize, the wooden spoon, but Alan couldn't even find a sarcastic 'Thanks.'

'Anyway,' she reflected, 'I wanted to know if he was as good as he was cracked up to be.' She was conciliatory now. She had said her piece.

'Was he?'

'What do you think?'

Alan smiled to himself. Before he had realised it she had picked him up off the deck and was putting his thoughts in order again.

'Is it true what Jeffrey said about Madeleine?' Despite all she had said, she sounded genuinely concerned.

'Yup.' He felt rational now, more able to look at the facts. 'Well, you know we split up, but I didn't tell you that part of it, that the "other man" was someone from the opposition. She told me about him when we had the row, apparently they met at the Yorkshire conference. I never thought for a moment ... huh, that's what they all say, isn't it? "I never thought for a moment." Anyway, I never suspected she was shacking up with somebody else. I just felt crucified. Up there, you know, with the nails through my hands and not even a chance of a spear with a wet sponge on the end.'

'I'm sorry.'

'Perhaps that's why I hunted Bishop so hard. One hard-nosed loud mouth's much like another.'

'Was Madeleine's man a loud-mouth?'

'I don't know. I just imagined he was. With short, stubby fingers.'

'There you go.'

'Huh, yes, there I go. Maybe it's helped, though, the thought that time wounds all heels. Death doesn't worry me much now. To be honest I'd be glad if the whole lot has been wiped out up there. I wouldn't like to think they'd got away with it.'

'Well, I don't want to die.'

If the words came as a surprise to Alan it was because, as she had said, he had been giving her too little thought. If that was what she wanted most of all, then that was what he wanted for her, too.

'No,' he said. 'I don't want you to die either. I wish I could see you smiling,' he said.

'Smile,' Beat said obligingly.

'Hmmm, sounds more like the gritting of teeth.'

'Are you surprised?'

'Where does it hurt?'

'Well, apart from the headache brought on by the thought that the whole world has just disappeared, my throat feels like ground glass in the bottom of a public lavatory, I've got scratches down my leg that sting like buggery, these sodden lumps of worsted tied around my ankles weigh a ton and if it isn't dragging up the past too much, I'd give my right arm for a glass of water and a hot bath. That's all. How about you?'

'Well, if you think that's bad, my bound hands have suffered the torture of a thousand cuts, my body is caked in sweat so thick the pores can't breathe, my eyes ache so much trying to see in the darkness that I'm convinced I'll go blind, and on top of it all there's a spot on my shoulder that I've been longing to pick all day and I know it's just growing and growing.'

'A spot! You think you've got problems with a spot? I've

been dying for a pee for more than an hour and I can't face the thought of baring my bum to the jaws of the rats. And to make matters worse, I keep seeing cans of Coke drifting by.'

'But that's marvellous. Grab one for me.'

'It's not marvellous, I hate Coke. The very sight of it gives me toothache.'

It helped, it all helped. The stories topped each other on into the early hours, fending off the fear of death, a death which nobody in the world would ever witness or have the worry of caring about. The possibility was not just all around them. It was creeping under their skin.

Tel and the girl were long past fearing the worst. This was the worst. And the worst for Tel as he sat alone with the girl in the back of a car – a different one now, one they had crept into at the edge of Hyde Park on the opposite side of Wellington Place to where the police officers had ended their escapade – the worst about the present was the future and the past. His family, his friends, the streets and institutions, the foundations of both his physical and emotional life, had vanished. No more Sunday lunch, no more West Ham, no more drinks with his mates, no more social security. The roots had been severed and there was nothing left he could point to to show what had shaped him, what had made him kick out, what had made him embrace, what had secretly conspired together to make him think, talk and act the way that he did. What made him Tel. Everyone now was the child of a bigger experience and there were no small excuses left any more.

The only slim thread linking him back to the past was the girl whose head was cupped in his lap, her eyes closed, her breath short but steady. She could take him back to a time when trains rattled along carrying people where they wanted to go, a time when girls could be smiled at and games could be played. There were no timetables now, no rule books to play by or try to cheat against. He brushed his fingers through the corn-stubble of her hair and it felt unexpectedly soft. Her sigh was deep and tremulous, like the whinny of a horse. Though exhaustion pricked drily at their eyes and smoky dust clung to their throats, neither could struggle across the threshold into sleep.

'Silly, isn't it?' she said. 'You spend half your life waiting to grow up and when you get there they take it away.'

'What did you want to be?' Their mouths desert-dry, they both spoke in whispers.

'Oh, rich, famous, in love. Ordinary things like that. What about you?'

'I don't know. It's two years since I was at school and I've never been able to get a proper job. I'd have liked to have – nothing special, but just to have shown I'd done something, I don't know, something useful. The money would have helped and all. I could have had a car and gone out a bit. Maybe even had a foreign holiday. Some of my mates have been to Spain and they really rate it. But I fancy New York.'

'I've always fancied Rome.'

'You got family?'

'Just my mum. I live with her down in Croydon. She's had a rough time ...'

The girl's voice trailed off and in the pause Tel imagined her thinking about the past. Just as he had done when he had stood staring at the smoke and fire that crackled over the spot where his brother had been.

She said: 'I never knew my Dad. He walked out just after I was born and Mum never saw him again, though she still talks as if he's coming back. She's a bit shy, so she hasn't got many friends. None, really. I wish I could phone her. She'll be ever so worried.' She sucked at her thumb.

'Have you got a feller?'

She shook her head, rocking it along his thighs.

'Why not?'

'I don't know. Too choosey, I suppose.'

That was the first impression Tel had had of her, on the tube, when she had loftily swung her head away from his grin. Too choosey by half. He could see it now, her living at home with a woman shut up with a bitter memory of a bloke who had cut and run. He would lay odds that when the old girl talked about 'men' she made it sound as if they came from another planet. In any other circumstances he wouldn't have stood a chance with the girl. It had taken the unnatural selection of doomsday to get her here, with her head in his lap. Or maybe she was like that with them all, prickteasing, then running away like her Dad.

'Do you regret it?' he asked.

'What?'

'Being choosey. I mean it might have been better if you'd been choosey afterwards, when you'd found out, like.'

'I'm not ...' She opened her eyes and looked up at the silhouette of his face and he thought for a moment she was going to say she wasn't that sort of a girl. Instead, she said: 'I'm not a virgin, you know.'

'That's one regret out the way, then.'

'Not really ...' her voice trailed off. 'The first time was when I was twelve. My uncle. It wasn't exactly pleasant.'

Tel didn't know what to say. She began to tell him about the experience. The way it came out, in gushes and hiccups as she felt for the right words, her story sounded unrehearsed, untried, as if she had never told anyone about it before, revealed her sense of guilt and humiliation. The revelation made Tel uneasy.

Then she reached up to discover the feel of his face. 'I'd like to kiss you but I'm frightened for my face. It's still burning hot and I don't want my skin to come off any more.'

'That's all right.' Romance had already fled from his mind. So had desire. In a gesture as much compassionate as sensuous he reached out to touch her breast through the wool of her jersey.

The yellow-green hands of the travelling clock said it was just after a quarter to three. Shirley stretched herself as much as she dared so as not to wake Simon. From the camping equipment which John, not without some foresight, kept in the cellar, they had taken the sleeping bags but there was nothing to cushion the effects of the floor except for the pillow she had made of the jacket she had been wearing when she first heard the news. In the cold damp of the night she had been kept warm by the boy who was sleeping in the bag with her. It was a tight fit but in the end, way past his bedtime, it had been the only way to get him to sleep. Despite the discomfort, with him asleep and Jack pitched at the foot of the stairs, the time alone was to be savoured. Marginally refreshed from the few hours' sleep she had come out of, she was fully conscious, listening to the occasional note of a symphony by Elgar which found its way through the crackle of the radio. It was not Jack who had got it working; it had come to faint life of its own accord during the course of the evening, the BBC's Wartime Broadcasting Service telling them what they wanted to know about the device that had fallen on London, the extent of the damage, the state of the country. They were to do nothing except stay where they were and leave their radios on.

The same thoughts she had left behind her when she fell asleep now returned with increasing anxiety. Were Jenny and John still alive and, if they were, were they also trapped in some dark, trouble-filled pit? The thoughts haunted, demanding answers, until finally, overwhelmed by them, she eased Simon to one side and slid from the bed. Gently removing the coat from under his head she slipped it over her shoulders and groped in the dark for her shoes. When she found them she picked them up and tiptoed barefoot over what she knew would be an unimpeded path to the bottom of the stairs. Her right foot creaked on the first step and a muscular hand completely encircled her ankle.

'Where are you going?'

'To find my daughter.'

'No you aren't.'

'You can't stop me.'

'I could come with you.'

The threat was easy to make. Of course there was no question of leaving Simon alone, just as there was no question of taking him out into the unknown night.

'But whatever's in the atmosphere,' Shirley protested, 'we'll breathe it in here. We haven't any air filters. All the oxygen is being constantly replaced.'

'I know, but there was something else out there today – the ash. That's not getting into the house, except round some of your broken windows. I don't know how lethal it is but it doesn't look healthy. Let's leave it until tomorrow.'

She sat down on a step and he released his hold. There was

a rustling of paper and his face was illuminated by a match he put to a small tipped cigarette. Holding the match away from him he looked at her until it burned out.

'What's up, can't you sleep either?'

'No.'

'Not nice in here, is it? No furniture, no windows. Like being in chokey. Bring us the candle over, will you?' When she didn't move he said: 'All right, I'll get it.'

There was the sound of the zip sliding back and the quilt being shrugged off and as she waited for his figure to appear in the candlelight she wondered if he ever had really been in prison before. When his silhouette did take shape beside the mop of Simon's hair there were no ragged edges to it; he was quite naked. Unperturbed, he turned and walked back to her, scratching his belly, and he placed the candle on the floor between them before climbing back into his bed. Apologising about the old man, he explained how he had first seen him in the hole in the road.

'Tough bugger he was, too. You wouldn't have known it to look at him. It was a good job you were here.'

'You might think so.'

'I do. And I'm grateful to you.'

'Oh, God.' Shirley suddenly hid her head in her hands and sobbed. 'It was awful.'

With Simon around all day, they hadn't talked about the incident, just cleared up, Shirley throwing herself into scrubbing the blood from her clothes, the floor, everywhere it had sprayed, and looking after her son, giving him the constant attention he demanded. Jack said nothing now and the tears flowed for nearly five minutes without comment. When they began to ebb and she felt her chest ache from dragging the terrible feelings up from deep within her, she opened her eyes to see that Jack was no longer there. Then she sensed him towering above her and she looked round. Bending down he was offering her something in his hand. She shrank back.

'You wash, I'll dry.' His large mouth spread in a smile as he took a paper towel from among a fistful of them and dabbed at her face. Through the blur of her tears she could now see he had an old paint sheet wrapped around him and she tried to smile, too, taking the paper towel from him to mop the last sniffs away.

'Will you be all right here?' The thick eyebrows furrowed with concern.

'What do you mean?'

'I'm just going over to the school.'

'But you said ...'

'I know. What's your surname? What class is Jenny in?'

Shirley told him and with a nod he stepped past her and made up the stairs towards his ash-covered clothes.

At first it was hard to know what the noise was. The pattering could have been mortar crumbling from the sewer roof, or it may have been a rodent army on the march. Alan and Beat listened to it, curious, wondering if it was just a trick of the senses, a confusion of the night. Then, from ahead, came the sound of footsteps in haste and the flickering of John's light.

'Come on,' he called before he had reached them. 'We've got to get out of here.'

'What's up?' Alan asked.

'It's raining.' He approached them. 'A large amount of the fall-out will have settled by now and the rain will bring it all down here. Whatever it's like outside we're better off there.'

Alan went to wake Bob. They didn't have to be told to leave this black, stinking place twice.

10: MORPHINE

As the night wore on, the flats on the Bessemer Park Estate began to fill up. Following the example of the first four women, others had come forward, one by one, until the entire estate was an enormous hospital with no wards, no nurses and precious little help beyond human comfort. Down the service roads between the blocks, amplified in the slim spaces between the rows and overwhelming the muddy grassed squares was the sound of the suffering. Many wondered if ever, in the rest of their lives, it would go away. Teachers at the nearby infants school arranged for some of the local children to spend the night in the Bingo hall to keep them away from the sight and the sound of the misery. Others stayed, being helpful, running errands, fetching water, candles, bandages and food. Some of the older ones even helped to carry away the dead.

In spite of the road blocks, some supplies were reaching Spennymoor. The young driver with his Citizen's Band radio was partly responsible, his jargon coming like an enthusiastic television commentary from his van parked by the Estate's football pitch. But other lorries and commercial vehicles, carrying what their drivers believed might be invaluable goods, had made their way towards the scene of the disaster and despite the curfew and threats enough were getting through to cause heavy congestion. As soon as anybody thought of it, the loads were divided, those considered not immediately essential being sent to the Trading Estate to wait, those needed to the football pitch, which glowed in the light of a bonfire fuelled with unwrapped cartons and boxes. If it had not been for the congestion, many drivers would have volunteered to go on to Durham but, as it had turned out for the student in the water lorry, they found their way blocked. Some turned their vehicles round and began asking anybody they could find where the back roads were to the city but it was a desperate attempt, a foregone conclusion that they would not get through.

Few people in the town slept. In the health and sports centres the helpers fought down tiredness which came on like nausea. If they had dropped on their knees they knew they would only be shaken awake by a new arrival or an old one with new problems or pains. In the surgery MacGilvray was closing the eyes of a woman who had died. The only thing she had said since she had been brought in about half an hour before was: 'They made such a noise, the cathedral bells, when the tower fell down.' A tea-shop apron clung to her in tatters and her face was brown; another patient from the Dryburn. As yet there had been nobody he knew well and it was hard to know how thankful to be.

There had been suggestions from the council that the bodies be disposed of down an old mine shaft to avoid the upsetting sight and the smell of mass cremation, but it was essential bodies were burned quickly to put off the day when cholera, diphtheria or typhoid would appear. The doctor took the ring from the woman's wedding finger to add to the boxful of personal items in the corner that one day people might come to identify. As it landed among them a voice came from the door.

'Who's in charge here?'

Without looking up to see who it was, MacGilvray said simply: 'God.'

When he did look round he saw the lieutenant, a young man with neat hair and a thin, dark moustache. In his hands was the mask he had now taken off but otherwise he was still in his protective clothes. It was a strange contrast to the doctor's butcher's apron.

'Sorry, I ...'

'Outside.'

'I just wanted a word with you, sir.' He began backing out of the door.

'There's a small office over there.'

The doctor followed him between the patients in the hall. It was valuable time, all such valuable time. Pushing in through the door of the cupboard-sized room they startled the young doctor who was supping a bottle of brandy. Without saying anything MacGilvray held out his hand and the young man handed it over.

'Just a fortifier, doctor,' he said sheepishly.

MacGilvray grunted and looked at the label. Then he took a mouthful himself, slooshing the liquid round his teeth, and handed the bottle to the lieutenant. He declined.

'We've brought some supplies, but there's a shortage of morphine, I'm afraid.'

MacGilvray stared at him. 'What about the emergency stocks, the ones the Home Office has been filching out of the NHS budget every six months for the past ten years or so?'

The lieutenant seemed more embarrassed than annoyed that he should be interrogated like this. 'According to the Ordnance chaps they've released some of it but most of it's going down to London. There's a stockpile in Newcastle we can't lay our hands on. All Tyneside's a no-go area because of the radiation but there have been reports that it may have already gone into Gateshead.'

'Well that's something. But get this straight, laddie, when your chums are making their wee plans for World War Four, make sure every town and city in this country has enough morphine for the entire population.'

The lieutenant bristled at MacGilvray's attack but the younger doctor stepped in to prevent further argument.

'What about the 100,000 beds they keep empty in America for their service casualties in Europe? Can we use them?'

MacGilvray's eyes opened wide. It was clearly the first time he had heard of it but to the lieutenant, scratching his head, it was old news.

'The Americans are still on red alert. But I think I've got a blood transfusion unit for you.'

MacGilvray nodded. It was a small compensation.

'It should be here in the morning, fully staffed. You understand that blood's in very short supply, of course.'

The young doctor suddenly laughed. 'God, it's like a "Boo, Hooray" game. The supplies have arrived – *hooray!* But there's no morphine – *boo!* There's some in Newcastle – *hooray!* But we can't get at it – *boo!* There are 100,000 empty hospital beds in America – *hooray!* But we can't use them – *boo!* There's a blood transfusion unit coming – *hooray!* But there isn't any blood – *boo!* Boo bloody hoo hoo.'

He slammed his fist against the wall. MacGilvray looked at

him, not in anger at the outburst but more in wonder, a wonder what to do with him. The younger doctor took a deep breath and shook his head in a deep shudder. 'I'm sorry. I'm tired.'

'See if you can find yourself some coffee.'

'Yes.' He walked out of the room.

When the door shut the lieutenant said: 'Is he ...'

'He's fine. Now what else did you have to tell me?'

'I've persuaded them to let me take a unit into Durham tomorrow afternoon – well, it's this afternoon now.'

Ignoring the irony, MacGilvray said: 'Hoo-bloody-ray.'

11: RUMOURS

In Chelsea, more than five miles from the blast, the landscape resembled an unchecked urban tip, and it was beginning to smell as bad. The tops of the buildings had been shaken off; roofs, chimneys, turrets, balconies and much of the ornamentation that had given character to the older houses lay in the pavement dust along with slabs of window-ledges, wrought-iron, splintered glass and the occasional gnarl of ivy that had clung to the centuries-old walls.

To the west the seven stumps of the council's proud red-brick World's End blocks of flats were half the height they had been a day ago, their jagged tops a spectre of a medieval fort that might have guarded a route out of town. Under the achromatic early-morning sky the whole scene was sullied as if every artist who had ever lived there had spilled his dirty water on it. Nor was the nearby river that many of them had painted ever to be the same. The power-station chimneys at Fulham, Lotts Road and Battersea were down, and all the craft that could float had long since begun their battle against the ebbing tide to take the city's refugees up the river. Chased by fire or panic and with no opportunity or wit to have second thoughts, those who took the plunge without a vessel quickly perished in water more deadly than all previous pollution could have made it. Now and then bloated bodies floated by, alone or in clumps, some beyond all recognition, slipping down the shrinking river towards the sea. In the slime of the widening banks of mud which was blistering from the thudding radioactive rain, some were beached; their removal would be left to the following tides.

Despite the rain and the high level of fall-out, there was activity. In King's Road cars had been heaved aside to release fire engines from Chelsea fire station and they crept forward in frustrated haste towards the beaconing flames. Sometimes, in their impatience, cars would be smashed from their paths, for though several bulldozers had been commandeered from building sites, they were not yet working in tandem with the brigade. Among the obstacles was the junk of collapsed buildings where small posses gathered, defying both the dangers and the official edicts, to dig with what makeshift tools they could towards the cries of the trapped which rose from the ruins. Meanwhile, along the main roads, Fulham, King's and the Embankment, the escapers trudged desperately, inexorably westwards.

In Chelsea Manor Street, between King's Road and the river, there was no sign of life until a manhole cover beneath a lorry heaved open, and banged to the ground, the sound muted by the pantechnicon's cavernous belly. Careful of the protruding back axle, the four from the sewer crawled out one by one, each immediately startled by the chill of the early morning which they sniffed as if it were a sweet Highland dawn. Like waking dogs they blinked and scratched and looked at each other. It was Saturday morning and they were back in the land of the living. Beat looked round her, squinting, getting used to the shadows, the shape of the light. Then she let out a yelp of a cry.

'What is it?' Alan stretched out an arm to her.

'Nothing.' She was shivering. 'I thought I saw a rat.'

'Bloody hell, look at that.' There was still a sparkle in Bob's eyes though they were red and piggy above his puffed cheeks. He was grasping at the shreds of material bound round his ankles. 'Teeth marks. The little buggers, they've been trying to take advantage of my young flesh while I was asleep.'

He tore away at the cloth and began inspecting his legs and ankles for tell-tale cuts in his skin, but there were none; only the material had provided food for the hungry rats. The others followed suit, gratefully shedding their sodden burdens that no longer bore any resemblance to the strips of smart clothes they had once been. Alan also removed the partly unravelled shirt tails from his hands. In the dull light the wounds from his frantic digging didn't look too bad.

'Where are we then, General?' Bob asked.

John had been peering out from under the lorry. His face was still drawn and pale around the thin dank wisps of beard; there were several more miles to go before he would feel he had survived.

'Chelsea Manor Street,' he said. 'About two hundred yards from King's Road.'

'Great. Nothing like a spot of cruising down here on a Saturday. What's the weather like?'

'Raining. Hard to tell how long it's going to last.'

More than the weather, the buildings around them had been occupying John's attention. The small row of shops alongside the lorry were mostly intact. Their plate-glass fronts, it was true, had joined the breakwaters of tiles and bricks along the pavement but they were still sturdy, their four walls standing up. It was a good sign.

'We'll try to find shelter until the rain's gone. Up on the right is a big block of flats. We'll have to be quick.'

And he was gone, rolling out from under the lorry with his briefcase held protectively on his head, getting to his feet and sprinting away. Bob downed the last of his Scotch with a grimace and scrambled out after the others.

To John, running was a wild relief. Each step instinctively found sure ground as he danced this way and that. To his left occasional shadows of figures, dead or sleeping, lurked in the jam of cars but he did not stop to see. There was only the driving sensation of speeding forwards, making time move again, and in vain he tried to go fast enough to feel the wind on his face. Turning into Swan Court, he gave only a passing glance up at the building that had stood nine-storeys high. About seven of them remained. Finally, in the arch beneath the crossbar of the H which shaped the block, he came to a stop, resisting the urge to breathe deeply, and listening to the pounding of his willing heart. There he recalled his nights of orienteering, the times he had pitted himself against nature and the clock and he thought, dammit, if it weren't for Shirley and the children I might actually enjoy this game.

He had tried the entrance doors on each side of the arch and found them locked by the time the others caught him up. It was strange to see the three of them in daylight. Alan seemed taller, more impressive looking, with grey streaks at his temples and a slight air of self-importance that was lost from his voice in the sewer. Beat, who Alan was shepherding forward, was less attractive than he had imagined, and a few years older. Still, the character that had emerged in the darkness was highlighted on her puffy morning face. Bob, on the other hand, who was now hurling a brick at a terrier that was yapping at the feet of the running group, was just as he had thought, a short, dumpy figure packed with jokes. None of them was really John's type of person, but then who was? Family apart, he needed few people in his life and amid all this catastrophe his single feeling had been merely that the human race, a species of highly gregarious animals, was being threatened with extinction. In his will to live he saw himself as no more than another animal struggling for survival.

When Alan reached the arch he asked, 'Can't we go inside?' and John detected that in the daylight, in more familiar surroundings, the man would not be content to be led for much longer.

'Doors are locked.'

'Let's try a bell.' Alan scoured the tiers of oblong buttons alongside the intercom and picked a low number in the hope that the occupant would be nearby. When there was no reply he tried another, then another.

'Who is it?' The woman's voice that eventually croaked through the mesh box was posh and demanding.

'There's four of us,' Alan announced. 'It's raining and we'd like shelter for a few hours.'

'Come up,' she commanded. 'I'm on the second floor. Make sure the door's closed behind you.'

A buzzer sounded and they let themselves in. The stairs were empty, the corridors midnight quiet and the air was tinged with smoke. On the second floor a door stood ajar.

'Come in, come in.' The woman's appearance was marginally less formidable than her voice. Past sixty, she was not tall, but she had a ramrod back, silver hair unfurling from a bun and a face slightly parched from years of sitting in the sun. But there was a paleness to it that wasn't hidden by make-up. All the lined curtains in the small flat were drawn, blacking out the sunless day. They were ushered into a room lit by a Victorian brass oil lamp. It was enough to show that the paintings on the walls were original, that the porcelain on the yew sideboard wasn't won on a Blackpool rifle range and that the rugs on the floor were from the East. If he had been dressed in his best suit, John would have still felt out of place.

His discomfort wasn't helped when the woman said: 'God, what's that smell?'

'I'm afraid we were stuck in a sewer,' Alan explained with a wry smile that made John think he was used to trying to get people on his side. 'Since yesterday lunchtime.'

'You poor things,' she said. 'You must be starving.'

'A bit parched.' Bob said and, to his own apparent surprise, he broke wind. 'Pardon me.' He patted his stomach. 'It's been hell in there.'

'We're not to touch the water,' she said. 'But I've got a few tonics left.'

From the sideboard where a near-empty bottle of gin stood, she took four small bottles and handed them to Bob to distribute. They accepted them eagerly, not speaking as they swigged away. John took his slowly, swilling a mouthful from cheek to cheek and feeling the bubbles going off like jumping jacks. He didn't want to drink it all. He wanted to keep some for his briefcase, just in case. But he was, he realised after the second mouthful, very thirsty indeed.

Apologising for being out of bread, the woman produced a packet of Bath Olivers before turning her attention to Beat.

'My dear, you must feel perfectly dreadful. My bedroom's through there. Your young man' – she was referring to Alan – 'can fetch a pan of water from the bath. We must be a little sparing, so use my cold creams. Perfume, too. Make yourself smell nice, it's always so important. You're not quite my size but do help yourself to absolutely anything you like from my wardrobe.'

Beat thanked her and went into the small hallway to find the bedroom, to be followed not long after by Alan carrying a pan of water and a dustbin liner for her old clothes. The door closed behind him.

Suddenly finding himself facing the woman, John said almost by way of apology: 'We won't bother you for long. Just until the rain stops. Midday at the latest. The fall-out should have mostly settled by then.'

'Stay as long as you like,' she said. 'Nobody has any rights to property any more. Those who have ever owned any know that it isn't really theirs, they're just borrowing it for a while. Well, I think the leases are up, don't you?'

'I ... I'm not sure.' John thought of his own home, so hard won, so carefully fitted out. Even guests made him jumpy, the way they didn't understand how things worked, where things lived. He would regard any intrusion like the one they were perpetrating on this woman as an abuse and a violation.

'In that box over there' – she pointed to where Bob had found himself a perch – 'is several thousand pounds' worth of silver. Chockablock. It's no earthly good to me and half of it is so tasteless I wouldn't dream of putting it out. But we accumulated it over the years, my late husband and I, as an investment. Nobody knows about it, though, except my daughter. That's her, with her three children.' A colour photograph of a vivacious young woman and three extravagantly healthy children sitting by a swimming pool stood on a bookcase. 'Super girl, she's in Canada. When I die, I've told her, she's got to come here straight away and get it out of here. It's not insured, you see. Otherwise it would show up on the probate.'

Bob chuckled, but John had other things on his mind. 'What's actually happened?' he asked. 'We've been in the sewer since the warning. We don't know.'

'My dear, I don't think anybody does. There are lots of stories, of course. Sit down, sit down. Don't mind the furniture.'

John nevertheless picked up a newspaper and spread it out on the green velvet settee before allowing his body the luxury of sinking into its curves.

'As a matter of fact you were rather lucky to get in,' the woman went on. 'There has been a little party organising the building. I expect they have fallen asleep. After the first rush just before whatever it was went off the front doors have been kept under firm lock and key. There were casualties here, the poor people on the top floors. A few small fires, too. Anyway I've kept out of it. I've just said that the flat's here if anybody wants it, otherwise everyone seemed to know what they were doing. I'm quite willing to help but one can't keep saying so all the time. There are a lot of *organisers* in this block of flats; you know, the type who won't talk to you from one day to the next but are frightfully good at knowing what's best when you ask their advice.'

John found it hard to know if she were sober or if the gin bottle had been recently emptied. It was difficult to tell sometimes with the rich. 'But what happened,' he asked, 'with the bombs?'

'Well, according to our helpful boy-scout troop, one has gone off in the city, one in the North Sea, two in the north of England and one in poor old Scotland, though how they know is a mystery. My radio hasn't been working since this all began. Are you any good at electrics?'

John shook his head. 'The radio flash probably destroyed a transistor or two. Do they know how the explosions were caused?'

'They're "looking into it". Every time I hear that phrase I think of ostriches with their heads stuck in the sands.'

'It's very odd. Five bombs don't make a nuclear attack and judging by the damage the one in London wasn't very big. Nothing an aircraft would have brought.'

'Are you an army man?' It was as though she were addressing a cocktail party guest.

'No, but when I was at school I was active in the CND.'

'Good for you. I think we all should have done a little bit more.'

'Morris? That's the name of a car, not a dog,' Shirley remembered John saying to a new neighbour when being introduced to his shaggy, two-tone mongrel. She recalled, too, the neighbour's reply: 'I bet there are more Rovers with four wheels than four legs.' The worrisome noise from the top of the stairs, the persistent scratching and continual whine which had been going on since she and Simon had sat down to a candlelit breakfast, undoubtedly belonged to Morris. It was disturbing the carefully-arranged meal which was designed to continue the lost routine and Simon had begun shouting for the dog to be let in. Since Jack had left, Shirley had found no more sleep, sitting through what she supposed must be the dawn with a deepening concern for Jenny and John, imagining a future both with and without them. Now and then memories of the past day came back to her like dreams suddenly recalled: the explosion, the old man's rage, the wandering, naked figure of Jack. Sometimes they made her weep, sometimes they just seemed rather bizarre. It had been nearly five hours since he had gone to the school and she kept recalling how he had said he had not liked to be cooped up here, and she wondered if he might never come back.

In the end she shouted back at Simon, giving as good as she got. 'All right, I'll give the bloody dog something to eat but he's not coming in here.'

'I want to see him.'

Angrily she took a handful of biscuits from a tin. 'But you stay down here; just stay where you are and don't you dare move.'

Her rage left Simon shouting defiantly as she stormed up the stairs. Expecting the dog to make a dash into the cellar, she eased the door open slowly, letting in the first daylight for nearly twenty hours. The dog backed off, his head low, whimpering. The fawn and dark brown coat was almost black, the hairs wet and matted and the long tail which should have flapped gratefully hung limp. 'Biscuits?' Shirley tossed them down on the carpet in front of him and he cocked his head at the sound of their fall. His eyes, she now saw, were opaque and useless and she could not resist feeling sympathy as she picked one of the biscuits up off the floor and held it in front of his salivering mouth. There was no telling what had happened to the neighbours, to his master or the friend who had first phoned to give her the news. The front door was just ajar, the catch down, and in the messy kitchen at the back of the house, vandalised in the haste of their departure, she could see the back door wide open, the windows stained grey. Rain was coming into the house through the skylight above the stairwell and it thudded against the broken glass that glinted on the carpet a few feet from her. The sound of dripping water came from upstairs. In spite of all this she wondered if she might make a quick tour to see if there was anything to ease their time in the cellar – games for Simon, cologne and a brush for her hair, books for them all.

Looking into the kitchen, wondering if there was something they had missed there, she suddenly thought she saw a scrap of tinfoil on the floor move. When she stood up to see what it was, it made a dash towards her. Its thick body was about nine inches long, its long coat reddy-brown. It had a snub nose, short, thick ears and a tail almost the length of its body. But all Shirley saw at first was a blur as the creature leaped and landed, continuing its headlong advance a few feet away. In a second the dog was yelping in pain and his head flung furiously round to one of his hind legs where he buried his own teeth into the painful bite. Fearful of what the rodent might do next, Shirley clutched at her hair, already imagining the paws starting to climb her, the grip of its four- and five-fingered feet.

Hastily retreating into the cellar she tripped on the paint-sheet Jack had discarded, falling down the first of the stairs and knocking her head against the unplastered wall. In the confusion and the struggle to get to her feet she could not be certain, and she had to keep blinking to make sure. It was too great a risk to believe that it wasn't true.

'Why did you fall over?'

'Don't move!'

Getting to her feet she first climbed the few steps to slam the door shut on the simpering dog, then ran back down the steps, growing used to the candlelight again, to pick the boy up off the floor. Only in her arms would he be safe. In the other hand she picked up the candle and began kicking at the objects, dislodging the articles that had been so carefully tidied away. For a while Simon provided her with courage: it was he more than her who needed to be protected. Yet in the commotion he could sense her fear and he stayed quiet, clinging to her neck as she kicked her way through the room, overturning anything in her path, exposing every hiding place. It had not so far occurred to her just what she might do if the rat did suddenly appear: just finding it, chasing it out in to the open, seemed as much as she needed to do. The fleeting shadows cast by the candle were not much help and twice she had had to stand back and peer hard to see if the shadows would take on a solid shape. When the sleeping bags had been turned inside out and all the household goods had been kicked from the 'fridges' and 'larders' she picked all but two candles out of the box and arranged them round the room.

In the improved light she saw that there was only one place

she had not yet explored and that was among the camping equipment. Piled neatly in the corner where John had left it, it maintained an orderly air from the past, one that had once belonged to their home, and instead of lashing out at it she bent down, resting Simon on her knee, and began putting the items to one side, one by one – the peg bag, the food containers, the fuel for the Primus, the tent . . . At the bottom of the pile was a groundsheet, folded up, and as she lifted it from the floor not one but two rats ran out. It was impossible for her to hold back the scream that rang round the cellar and reduced Simon to immediate tears. Nor, in the shock of the moment, had she had time to see which way the rats had run.

Trembling and perspiring profusely, she was now determined she must destroy them before they destroyed her. It was as if all her fear and terror was now concentrated on the one enemy she could see, as if the rat held more true horror than the nuclear holocaust. Watchfully, she put Simon down, then picked up the tent-pole bag and opened it up, only to find herself near screaming again when a spider scuttled out, tickling its feet along the length of her fingers. Her heart pumped and her eyes were pricked with tears. The poles, pushed together, formed a long weapon and she lifted Simon into her arms again to take up the hunt once more. Now each stab at a drawer, a box, a cloth or a packet unnerved her. Each jab or prod might incite one or both of the hungry, sharp-teethed, diseased vermin and bring swift retribution – a searing bite on the leg or, with a rush and a leap of their prickly paws, a savage attack anywhere. At first the blows from the pole landed before such thoughts could cross her mind, but the expectation came more and more quickly, making her aware of the possible consequences of each blow before it was struck. Soon she was seeing in the shadows not one or two, but a mad, lemming-like rush of rodents and despite the smashing pole which had begun to splinter and break, she could no longer keep the shadows back.

Knowing that the poisoned dog, the fatal rain and perhaps more vermin awaited them, she fled up the stairs to the house, stopping only to close the cellar door behind her, and heading for the first floor and the bathroom, the one room she thought might be safe. Once inside she shut and bolted the door before looking around her. The window was intact; only the mirror that had hung over the sink had fallen down and smashed into the basin and across the floor, denying her the sight of herself in sorrow. Before she began clearing it up, she lowered the lavatory seat and sat down exhausted, Simon in her lap. Her body shook with tremors of panic and relief, and as she listened to the continued whine of the dog she wondered just how much more she would have to endure.

'Aren't you well?' Simon asked, mimicking the gentle voice she herself used when he was sick. 'Do you need some medicine?'

'Yes,' she sighed. 'Lots and lots of medicine.'

In the following hour Simon was kind to her, reasonable and comforting in a serious, adult way. He helped to clear up the glass then made her lie down on the lino while he 'looked after' her. But her mind repeatedly wandered from him, going back to the rats, to the house, to the neighbourhood, to the night and to the disaster of the previous day. Sometimes it would escape to a hidden void where there were no thoughts at all.

Jack's arrival was unmistakable – a roaring rebuke and a yelping of the already badly injured dog as it was driven from the house. At once, Shirley was on her feet, opening the door and shouting down the stairs: 'Don't go in the cellar. There are rats in there!' The dusty boots clumped up the stairs and he came along the landing towards her, a full carrier bag in one hand, a council road lamp in the other. He stopped in front of her and looked her up and down, but not in the way he had when they first met.

'Your girl's safe. They're all right, in the school, they've got things running like clockwork.'

Her shoulders slumped and she ran her fingers through her hair. Safe for what? What kind of life would they have now? Yesterday's explosion wasn't the end, it was the beginning of an existence that would never be far from death. Looking up at Jack, she suddenly had the feeling she was seeing Simon, grown up, and she half expected him to reach out and put his arms around her, to ask if she was all right, if she wanted some medicine. In his tired face was the same concern the boy had, the same look of surprise and pity. He turned away.

'I'll see about the rats, then,' he said.

But Shirley did not want him to go.

Tel had been watching the girl's face for some time: the wilting halo of spiky blonde hair; the plucked eyebrows flecked at the roots with brown; the soft skin pale, greying nearly, making her cracked lips look redder, more plush; the scarlet-nailed fingers clamped as if she was in deep thought just below her chin; and the whole dominated by the purple-edged black stain on her cheek. In sleep, curled up in the back of the car, she was quiet and her body was barely disturbed by its breathing.

Leaning over the back of the driver's seat, Tel held a half-drunk can of lager in one hand, a full one in the other. The vehicles had proved to be the nearest, if the least generous providers of sustenance and he had had to go no further than the boot of the Ford to discover the pack of four tins. There, too, was a grimy sheet of polythene he had draped over the girl to keep off the pattering rain that splashed in through the window frames. Around them the activity of Hyde Park had been quenched. Pockets of people huddled beside the remains of charred trees, looking out over the lying figures of those left in the rain, the ones who had not survived the night. Agincourt, Waterloo, Balaclava – their dead were these dead, all become one on the bleak fields of aggression. The only thing different now was the grey film that covered it all. That and the absence of victors.

For Tel it had been disturbing to wake to the destruction again, to see the smoke still pluming in the east and remember he would never see his family or friends again. Every morning would announce itself in the same way for a time, a familiar messenger knocking with the same bad news. The girl, though, she would help. She was the hope, like the strange shock of yellow daffodils he had noticed, careless and bright in the dust on the far side of Rotten Row. Perhaps the whole country would be turned into an agrarian society where every man had his work, every man had his choice. The idea of such a purpose; building, imagining, touching things that would come to life, brought him a sudden and unexpected flutter of happiness. Just him and the girl, starting together. But she would have to get better first.

He hadn't wanted to leave her in case she woke up and found herself deserted but, not long after waking, the call of nature had become too strong and he had slunk from the car and run to the nearest elm tree. Standing in the rain he felt the cuts on his feet come alive and he began recalling his search for Bob, wondering if he had done enough, when there came a small cry from the far side of the tree. Looking round it he saw someone so badly burned that their race and age were impossible to discern. With no hair on her head, only the remnant clothes showed that she was a woman. When she saw him, through eyes that had more white in them than should be, she held out her hand and begged him for water. It was then that he had returned to the car to find anything that might bring the slightest relief and it was there, in the boot, that he had discovered the cans. By the time he had returned, her head had slumped forwards and when, bending down, he gently pushed at her shoulder, he found no response. First the man in the Two Chairmen, now her. They seemed to be dying at his touch. Wiping his hand on his trousers he stood up and was about to hurry back to the car when a voice called out: 'Excuse me!' In the opposite direction a middle-aged man with no sign of injuries was coming towards him.

'She's dead. I didn't do anything.'

'They're all dying, son.' He was out of breath and there was perspiration like a moustache on his upper lip. 'We're starting to distribute to those that need most.' He pointed into the park, between defoliated trees, where Tel could make out the shape of a grandstand in which a sorry looking group were gathered. If there was anything to eat or drink there, it didn't show. He broke off two cans anyway.

'Half each. There's some people in the car who are thirsty. Do you know where I can find a doctor?'

'We haven't come across any yet.'

'Where are they taking the sick?'

'Nobody's taking the sick.'

The man was anxious to get away, and Tel stood for a minute watching him scuttle back towards the bandstand. He hated anybody calling him 'son'. Someone, somewhere must be doing something. As soon as the girl woke he would go into the streets and find out.

It was nearly an hour before she opened her eyes, seemed to fall back to sleep, then woke again. Her lower lip turned inwards and her two slightly protruding, milk-white front teeth scratched at it before her tongue came out to give it a wipe. Consciousness returned with a shudder. Tel shook the can, and her eyelids flicked back so she could focus on the tin and on Tel.

'Drink?'

She didn't answer at first, then she slowly sat up, looked about her and reached out for the beer. It went down slowly, checked by the intermittent swelling of her Adam's apple and it was only when it was all gone and she had handed the tin back that she screwed up her nose and said: 'Oooff!' She looked round the park, at the cars, at the damage. Finally she asked: 'What's the time?'

Tel looked at his watch. 'Quarter past two?' Its face was smashed and he would have thrown it away except it was a present from Bob.

She stared out at the park again and at the cars around her, then looked down at her body, brushing her jeans and jersey flat. Idly, her left hand went out and ran over the seat where she had been lying. It made a fist which she brought up in front of her face. One by one the fingers uncurled and Tel saw a small shower of light flecks fall to the floor. It took him a moment to realise that it was her hair. A small patch at the back of her head had fallen away.

'Is there a mirror?'

'I don't think so.' The rear-view had shattered but he tried the glove compartment, making more rummaging sounds than he need, to prove that there was nothing there. 'It's all right, your face. It doesn't look any worse than yesterday.'

She nodded as if it were of no great concern.

'I'm going to see what I can find out. There should be *some* hospital that's still working.'

Again she nodded and Tel reached over and gathered up the sheet of plastic she no longer needed. Turning his head he found his face next to hers, their eyes, their stale breath colliding. Without pressure he touched his dry lips along hers, like feather dusters. Watching her he sat back again.

'Don't go away,' he said for the second time in their brief acquaintance.

She managed a smile. 'I can't think of anywhere to go.'

He pulled the plastic sheet over his head and set off into the rain. Cars were thinner here. They hadn't bottlenecked as they had on the main road, though a number had piled up at the lights at Albert Gate. He had to make sure he was out of sight of her before he began searching for shoes. Brown brogues on a corpse slumped across the front seat of the third car he looked into seemed as if they might be about his size and he began to unfasten the laces.

'Oh, God,' the sudden moan made Tel stand back. Then: 'Where's Annie? Where's she gone?'

In his initial confusion, Tel thought he must be referring to the woman he had just seen die in the park, but the coincidence, he realised, would be too great. 'I'll look for her,' he promised. 'Let's just get you comfortable.'

He eased off the smashed glasses that hung from one ear, loosened his tie and finished taking off the shoes. But it wasn't until he had walked a few cars away that he pulled them on, only to discover they were on the large side and slipped off at the heel. Still, they were better than nothing and his feet were glad to be inside them. He was feeling tired now. Perhaps he had only had an hour or two's sleep; he should have tried to get some more. The shoes, like small rafts, took him up the black grass bank beside South Carriage Drive and down into Knightsbridge where the wrecked cars, bombarded by buildings, were jammed solid again. Occasionally a figure would scurry fast through the rain, otherwise there were only the dead. Climbing over the railing on to the pavement, Tel's feeling that he was in a ghost town was compounded by a murmur like the roar from a sea shell clamped on each ear, which entered the street in waves from his left. Though he looked for any sign of its source he could see nothing, only the cars, only the tumbled remains of Wellington House and the arch on which Boadicea once rode. What he did not know was that an underpass here took cars through to Piccadilly and it was crowded with those who were escaping the fire, the fallout and now the rain. The sound of the sorrow that huddled inside it was amplified through the tunnel like a giant megaphone. Instinctively Tel made his way in the opposite direction.

The Victorian piles lining the streets were in tatters, as if the Queen herself had been reduced to rags. None of the glass remained in the bare shop windows and at Harvey Nichols stripped dummies, pink and synthetic, were all that remained of the shop's displays. Where was everyone? What was going on? Tel didn't know this part of London at all and a claustrophobia came over him with the thought that the debris, the mess that kept him from the space of green fields, might go on for dozens of miles. He hurried past the shattered egg-box of the Sheraton Hotel, past the crushed green canopy that welcomed guests to the now hidden ballroom of the Hyde Park Hotel, until he reached the hotel's grand entrance. Behind its glass front doors people pressed, alive if barely moving. Outside, in the cover of the porch stood a liveried doorman, incongruously wearing a dusty black top hat and talking to a policeman in uniform.

Hurriedly, Tel scrambled up the pile of bricks that flanked the doorway, knowing that his first footfalls on the loose ground had made them turn to watch. At the top he stood up to face the policeman, a middle-aged sergeant with an old-fashioned expression that said little more than 'What's your problem, then?'.

'I've got a sick lady in the park,' Tel began.

The sergeant nodded and crumpled his lips in some kind of sympathy.

'Well, what's the form?'

'Everyone's sick, son. Keep her there if she's comfortable. It shouldn't be long before we get some help.'

Tel felt the heat of anger ignite in his stomach. 'But there must be doctors around. Even a bottle of aspirin. I'm not asking for much.'

'There's a doctor up on the third floor. But he's not making house calls.'

The remark seemed to make the doorman grin and, in a rage, Tel leapt past them and banged in through the doors, not listening to the sergeant calling out: 'Take it easy now, son.'

Inside, his impetus was immediately stopped by the crush, by the solid mass of a crowd, by the stench of sickness and diarrhoea.

'Hey, don't push.'

'What's your hurry?'

'I want to see the doctor.'

A young man his age, his arm bandaged by a shirt, pointed up to the two flights of stairs that led off in both directions at the back of the lobby. Tel looked out across the heads, some bald, some strangely misshapen, across the patches of flesh, blood and burns and up to the press of people on the stairs. The queue showed no signs of moving. Some were standing, many sat, adults moaned, children wailed.

'I've got a sick lady in the car.' The sentence was coming out automatically now, an *idée fixe* that was beginning to haunt him.

'None of us are too chipper.' An old man, blotchy-faced, was to his right.

'Well, what's going on? Where are the rescue parties?'

'I'm sure they're doing their best,' said a middle-aged man with no visible wounds.

'One bang in London doesn't put the whole country out.'

'There's been more than one.'

'What?' Tel kept turning, trying to catch the speakers.

'The whole of Britain's a desert.'

'Well, where are our allies? The Americans?'

'Late again. Like the last couple of times.'

'They've attacked Russia. Wiped it out.'

'The royal family's dead.'

'They've all got bunkers.'

'I thought they were supposed to take off to Canada.'

'There wasn't time.'

'God, I never thought Australia would sound attractive.'

The words went round, the eyesore of one injured face, then another, the smell of decay, of lives rotting where they stood. Round and round ... round and round until, in a spin like one induced by too much drink, Tel went round with them, bumping into those about him as he collapsed on to the floor.

12: RADNET

The BBC Wartime Broadcasting Service was now operating from its safe underground station at Evesham in Worcester and mobile transmitters had been brought across the Pennines in an attempt to establish contact with the devastated area of the north-east. Very high frequency signals were still disturbed by the explosions and there was no question of television transmission. Broadcasting on medium wave, the service was a supplement to local radios which still provided the most part of the day's reporting, dealing with specific problems in each area, the clearing of roads, warnings about fires and collapsed buildings and explanations of food and water distribution points. Appeals were for co-operation rather than help, since all help was being organised by the authorities and their recruits.

In Spennymoor, a large portable radio, its transistors intact and with sparkling new batteries, had been brought in to the council chamber early on Saturday morning. Activity in the room had continued all night, though by the morning many people had been affected by some kind of radiation sickness and had been sent home – if their homes were in town. Those that left were soon replaced by new arrivals with new problems but the room was not quite as full as it had been in the first hours. With the centres of help set up, the management of the many problems had been distributed. Ted Evans was still there, his tie undone, his shoes off. Councillor Greenhalgh and Maggie Blackett looked equally frayed.

When they first switched the radio on, all the news seemed to be local, although there was no mention of Spennymoor. The reports were entirely concerned with the difficulties rescue workers were having on the A1(M) to the east, and the spontaneous evacuation south from Sunderland, Seaham and Peterlee. There was now no hope, the reports said, for two hundred miners trapped in the flooded Vane Tempest colliery 1500 feet beneath the bed of the North Sea. Rescue work was continuing at the Dawdon, Easington, Hordon and Blackhall mines and only close relatives of the miners were allowed near the collieries where help was already hindered by congestion. The lifeboat had put out from Tees Mouth and the coastguards at Hartlepool repeated their warning that it was dangerous for anybody to set out to sea. The Duchess of Kent Military Hospital at Catterick in Yorkshire was now completely full and everyone was reminded that only in emergencies should medical treatment be sought. Minor injuries, nausea, vomiting and diarrhoea should be treated at home.

The long list of disasters, any one of which would otherwise have remained on the front pages of newspapers for days, was ended when the BBC's nationwide news round-up was broadcast at eight o'clock. It was read in an old-fashioned ponderous tone:

'The President of the United States has made a strong protest to the Soviet Union about a submarine attack on the US Navy cruiser Truxtan. *The cruiser, which was on its way to investigate the Polaris submarine* Resolution, *was severely damaged by three torpedoes fired by the unidentified submarine. Nato ships are in the area searching for the cruiser. Meanwhile* Resolution *is now lying alongside the British frigate HMS* Devonshire *where the commander has been taken on board.*

'As radiation from the five nuclear explosions in Britain drifts across the North Sea, evacuation has begun in the coastal towns of Belgium and Holland. Inland, people are being asked to stay in their homes and emergency supplies are already being distributed throughout the two countries.

'Here in Britain rescue services are in full operation but the government has repeated its warning that everyone not in the disaster areas should stay in their homes. The speed and success of the rescue operations depends entirely on clear roads and lack of interference, which has already caused delays in essential supplies reaching some parts of the devastated areas.

'A spokesman for British Gas says that fires from the North Sea gas fields caused by the explosion in The Wash are completely out of control. They will be left to burn themselves out. British and Norwegian helicopters are continuing their attempts to rescue the crews of North Sea oil rigs damaged by the

tremors from the explosion in Aberdeen.

'In London, the Prime Minister has been in touch by telephone with the Queen and we shall be broadcasting a message from Her Majesty later today . . .'

So, the Prime Minister was safe, the Queen was safe, the Polaris 'mishap' was common knowledge and there was a diplomatic row going on. Those gathered in the council chamber had hoped for something more positive, more reassuring. Their own town's supplies of water and medicine were spasmodic and their food stocks would not last forever. There had been no suggestion of the scale of the rescue operations nor any sign of real help. But perhaps there was nothing more to say; perhaps all they had was as much as anyone might expect. For Councillor Greenhalgh the news was an appetiser and he was anxious to know more of what was going on. He had already visited the signals unit lorry three times in the course of the night but they were either as ignorant as everyone else or they weren't letting on. He did, however, know the local radio ham and after the broadcast he went across the town to find him.

When he reached the garden hut where the ham housed the equipment, he found that he was not alone in his quest for more news. The ham was already talking to an enthusiast in Belgium, a retired clerk from the Supreme Headquarters Allied Powers in Mons, and the ham held one end of the earphones slightly away from his head so that the voice might filter out into the room. Greenhalgh bent down to listen.

'Here in Ypres we must take in one family each from the people evacuated from Nieuwpoort, a small town on the coast. They say we must live like this for about fourteen days. I think our economy will be ruined. We will not be able to eat anything grown here for many years. But of course it is worse for you. There are many boats now coming from England, many small boats trying to get here before the radiation, but how can they travel faster than the wind that blows them? Already there are many English sick in our hospitals. Your military authorities say they have stopped all ships leaving port, but the small boats are enough. There has been so much activity, you know, so many reports. We heard that your prime minister was dead, that an American nuclear depot in

Britain had exploded. Then I think they began to censor the news, especially after the problem with your bombers.'

'What bombers? We haven't heard about that.'

'No? Well, you have an RAF base at Waddington in Lincolnshire and there are Vulcan bombers there, yes? Nuclear bombers. Lots of aircraft took off when there was the warning – we had the warning here too. But your East Anglia was like a beehive when somebody throws a stone at it. English, American planes, we could hear them coming over the coast very low, terrible racket. But the Vulcans, we hear, four of them flew right into the bomb off The Wash. It is very lucky that their nuclear bombs did not detonate – if they were carrying them, of course.'

'What happened to the others?'

'I think they began to circle in the air before they reached the border, waiting for their "Go Code", but of course it never came and they landed or returned to Britain. But two of your Vulcans, they must have had some damage to their radio equipment and they just carried on flying. We think that this is what happened to the two American planes from Scotland, too, except that the Russians came out to say hello when they got to Finland. You know, when a pilot joins a squadron like this in Nato, he is given the name of a target in the East, so that when the attack comes he knows where to go. Well of course this is very dangerous, like Dr Strangelove. The pilot sees the bomb go off, perhaps his family is nearby, I don't know, and he just goes on and on until somebody tells him to stop. The Luftwaffe managed to persuade one of the Vulcans to come down in West Germany but the other one they had to shoot at. He came down over the border in Altmark somewhere.'

'What a carry on! That must have been nearly World War Three.'

'Oh no, no, no. On the radio now the American President is talking about making protests to the Soviet Union and so on, but really both sides know what's happening. They know the difference between a cock-up and an act of aggression and in a business like this you must get some cock-ups. You know, when they call each other up on their red telephones they will be saying "So sorry, Mr President", "My apologies to you, Mr

President, and my regards to your wife and I hope she is well."
They know what has happened to you in Britain and they are not quite mad enough to want it for themselves.'

'But what about the missiles? Why did they go off in the first place?'

'Another cock-up.'

After Belgium, they picked up a ham in Norway. From him they learned that the Norwegian and Danish governments had promised to take any refugees arriving by sea from the north-east. Small pleasure craft, fishing boats and flat irons as well as passenger and cargo boats had put out from Tyneside and Teeside to escape the radiation and the Scandinavian navies had spent the night answering distress calls and chasing flares from the ill-equipped vessels, some of which were sailing without lights and with damaged radio equipment. The Finnish government had lodged a protest with both the American and Soviet embassies in Helsinki about the dogfight which had occurred over its territory. The Nato countries were still on full alert and in Sweden the citizens of Stockholm had been preparing themselves to make for the capital's many shelters.

There was no response from hams around Newcastle and while they were trying to contact others in the area they were broken in on by a caller in Perth. After telling him their own situation, he gave them an idea of what was happening in Aberdeen. The bomb, which had evaporated the Torry district of the Granite City just south of the River Dee between the docks and the Shell complex, had instantly killed about half of the 200,000 population. In clean sweeps the emergency services came in from the north, from Inverness to Peterhead and down the coast, and from the south, from Perth and Dundee. Even the heavy fog did not seem to deter them. Ignoring the Home Office advice, the worst cases were taken to the hospitals and infirmaries throughout Scotland while the least injured were treated in field hospitals closer to the city. Balmoral had been personally offered to the Aberdeen victims by the Queen and some survivors were finding strange luxury surrounding their suffering. That was not to say that the problem was not still daunting enough but, in another refusal to follow the Home Office guidelines which stated that no rescue attempts could be made within fourteen days of an attack, there was already talk of sending working parties in.

This piece of news was greeted by Councillor Greenhalgh with some aggravation, since the army had already insisted not only that there could be no relief for Durham but that even here, in Spennymoor, help would be limited. His aggravation was not soothed when subsequent conversations with hams from Carlisle and Berwick-on-Tweed filled in the missing part of the picture: the picture of Newcastle, the capital of the north-east. Here, in the urban sprawl, the problem was proving far less easy to contain. The fires and damage from the bursts at Chester-le-Street and Durham had slaughtered the towns of Stanley, Birtley, Houghton-le-Spring and Washington, where the family home of the ancestors of America's first President had undoubtedly been consumed by flames. To the north fires felled the crowded tower blocks of Gateshead, to the east half of Sunderland was broken or in flames.

The docks had been scenes of fierce arguments not without violence, as people tried to board ships they thought might be sailing. It was only when the 15th/19th Royal Hussars were called out from Fenham Barracks and the message that no more vessels would be allowed to sail had been loudly and persistently broadcast, that the trouble began to die away. With no electricity, no water, no gas, and radiation blowing over the city, it was an impossible task to keep vast numbers of frightened people in their homes. Their escape routes were the A69 which cut through the Tyne Gap in the Pennines to reach Carlisle, and the roads north that led to the Scottish border. These roads had long since become completely impassable and only the faintest help was getting through from the west. Leaving their cars, their vans and their lorries, the refugees were joining others who had already set out on foot, to roam across the countryside up the Tyne and Derwent Valleys towards the Pennines. They roamed over the north, too, up the coast and over the Cheviots under the watchful eye of army helicopters, and the night had seen the valleys and the hills and the Northumberland beaches littered with the small fires of the thousands who had fled.

The news that all shipping out of Tyneside had been prohibited in spite of the Scandinavians' willingness to accept any 'boat people' compounded the frustration Councillor Greenhalgh already felt. But he had no chance to tell the district council what he had heard. While they were still talking with Carlisle the door of the shed was opened and an army sergeant with the red flash of the signals unit on his sleeve and two of the town's policemen crowded in. They had come to arrest the two men for using the radio set illegally.

Among those who had gone down with radiation sickness was the inspector and it was a police sergeant who brought the council news of the town's first arrests. It was clear that the only person who might be able to persuade the military authorities to let the men go was the chief executive, Ted Evans, and he was annoyed at having to leave the chamber. Maggie Blackett pointed out to him that apart from the army's communications lorry the radio was the town's only form of contact with the world, and therefore it might be worth taking care of. She mentioned that on his way to the police station Ted could call in to see his wife and family. Though a council worker had looked in on them once the previous day, to see that they were all right, Ted Evans had had no contact with them since a telephone call just before the warhead exploded. He needed no further persuading.

Outside, the sky was a clear, mocking blue and the sun was approaching its zenith with a brightness that seemed to say: 'Disaster? What disaster?' As he walked to the car park Ted Evans heard a loud explosion behind him and turned to see a plume of black smoke coming from the Green Lane Industrial Estate. Explosives had been brought in from the Coal Board depot at Tuxhoe to try to stop the factory fires from spreading any further. It was a strange feeling, to be moving, driving down into the town as if he were going home from work. But it was a different town. Everywhere curtains were drawn and the streets were free from all but the occasional car in a hurry. There were civilian officials on the streets and twice he was stopped and asked where he was going. His route through the centre of the town kept him away from the Bessemer Estate where there was most activity and evidence of the suffering, but he did pass by the end of the short road that led up to the health centre. Its doors were crowded with those waiting for news of friends and relatives, some of whom had brought victims in from Durham.

On the higher, south side of town he stopped in front of a tidy semi-detached house with lace-curtained bay windows and went quickly inside. His wife was upstairs in the boys' room. One of their sons was in bed. He looked pale and had been vomiting all night. Putting down the book she was reading to him, his mother, too, looked drawn. Like Ted, she had not slept all night. He sat on the bed and for a while talked to the two of them, telling them of what was going on in the town, finding out if there was anything they needed he might be able to get. Then he got up to leave the room.

'Where are you going?' his wife asked.

'To have a bath.'

She stared at him. 'What have you been doing up there all this time?'

His thoughts had gone out of gear and for a moment he had forgotten that the effects of the blast had hit his own home too, as well as the town he felt he was responsible for. He laughed at his own idiocy, and she suggested they went downstairs to the front room where a coal fire was burning and she could boil up some water for tea. There, he told her in more detail the problems Spennymoor faced and she asked if there had been any news of the people they knew in Durham. There had been none.

'We heard about the unexploded weapon.'

'Who told you?'

'Everyone seems to know about it. Is that why there has been so little help coming here? Are they afraid it might go off?'

'I don't know. I don't suppose it's very easy to bring in everything we need. The roads are terribly congested.'

'It's impossible to take it all in. What is it, a million, two million dead?'

'There's one consolation.' He smiled without humour. 'With the government's "stay-put" policy there are going to be a lot of people all over the country shut in their houses with nothing to do for a couple of weeks. By next Christmas the population will probably be back to normal again.'

The doorbell rang. It was a neighbour who had seen the car draw up outside and had come to ask for the news. It wasn't long before the man living opposite had come over, too. Everybody seemed to know about the unexploded warhead and, nearly twenty-four hours after the succession of people had walked into the council offices with the same question, everybody still wanted to know what was going on. Evans told them all he could and then made his excuses to leave before the whole street descended on the house.

Despite the continuous requests to stay off the streets, more than a dozen had found their way to the police station where they were queuing up for news of friends, demanding why they could not leave Spennymoor, complaining of minor problems that had sprung up in the town. Not wanting to throw his title around the chief executive stood for a moment among them, waiting his turn, until a policewoman came through a door behind the desk officer, complaining about the fuss the prisoners were making.

'Just because David Greenhalgh is a councillor ...' she began.

'I'd like to see them,' Ted Evans interrupted before she had a chance to say something she might regret. When he introduced himself, however, she was unrepentant and she asked him to wait while she fetched a detective. The police, the detective said, making no concessions to Evans' position, were entirely under the command of the army in York, and the orders had come to arrest whoever was using the equipment and anyone who was with him.

'But why didn't they just tell them to stop what they were doing? You could have even confiscated the radio. We've got problems enough with accommodation as it is.'

'Oh, we had to do more than remove the radio. Our orders were to break it up.'

13: MAKING PLANS

Of all the things Bob needed to have to prepare him for the day, a roll of bank notes was the most important. Each morning he would count it, tuck it into his inside top pocket and step out ready to face anything the world might have to offer. In his trouser pocket, where he had transferred it when he had torn up his jacket to bandage his ankles in the sewer, there was more than two hundred pounds, plus the forty-odd left from the fifty he had asked Tel to bring him. He hadn't needed the extra; he just wanted to give the kid something to do and by asking him to borrow some money off their dad, he thought it might make Tel feel he had earned the drink. But then look what had happened. Going back over it, as he had again and again, he knew that he hadn't really believed the warning, the idea that London was about to be blown away. That was why he had cheerfully gone back to fetch his briefcase from the bar. And then, when he reached the Two Chairmen and found the doors locked – in licensing hours – he suddenly knew it was serious and he had dived the wrong way, disappearing down the manhole like a rat. Whatever he had done for his brother in the past was now all wiped out by that one, cowardly decision. Angrily, he ground his teeth. Remorse wasn't something he had ever tried living with before but, sitting here in the darkened flat with his eyes closed as he drifted in and out of dreamless sleep, it was getting harder to make the memories go away. Opening his gritty eyes helped.

The old woman was sitting up at the table, jaundice-yellow in the light of the oil lamp. As she peeled over a pack of cards in a game of patience, she held her head back, examining each one the way a long-sighted reader does. On the sofa beside Bob, John looked alert even in sleep, ready to join any conversation that might suddenly start up. But conversation had stopped half an hour after their arrival, just after Alan had returned to the sitting-room and announced that Beat wanted to be alone. Beat was no Garbo, Bob had thought;

Alan must have been booted out. Now he slept, sprawled in a chair, pretending nonchalance. As Bob stood up he felt the pains in his shoulder and back where the bricks in the sewer must have pressed into him as he slept. The woman turned to see him.

'How's your luck?'

'It's coming out one time in thirteen.'

'Not bad.'

He wandered over to the window as the carriage clock was striking three. The rain had stopped but he wasn't about to wake John and tell him it was time to go home; he looked much too peaceful to disturb him. He pulled a corner of the heavy curtain back a few inches. Torn buildings stared back at him, dead cars lay silent in the street below. The bodies of people, more than a dozen in view, hadn't been moved and a Yorkshire terrier, the same one that had snapped at Bob's heels, was sniffing round one of them, licking its wounds. Bob wasn't very good with blood and he let the curtain drop back to turn his attention to the more attractive things closer to hand: to the porcelain, the leather-bound books, the pictures on the wall. When the others awoke they might want to be off, but he would be happier to remain here, where it was cosy – with the woman, her safe flat and her silver. He went over to watch her play. The cards flipped out of her hands in threes as fast as any croupier could deal and he guessed she had had to pass many idle hours either alone or with friends, abroad perhaps, where entertainment had to be home-made. When she came to the end of the deck she scooped all the cards up and began to lay them out again.

'How many times have you lost in a row now?'

'That makes twelve. It will come out this time.'

'Bet you a tenner it doesn't.'

She breathed in deeply, arching her back. 'Ten pounds probably won't buy us a loaf of bread by this time tomorrow.'

He remembered the write-offs out in the street. 'Have you got a car?'

'Yes ...'

'I bet you your motor against my house in Bow that you don't come out.'

'It's a deal.' The last face-up card went down and she

began matching them up, black on red, red on black. 'I must warn you that thirteen is a very lucky number for me.'

'And I think I should tell you that the chances of your coming out on the thirteenth game are about five billion-to-one – bloody hell, that's the fourth ace.'

With a practised eye that often made her hands move before Bob could see where the card was able to go, the lines of numbers built up. To make sure she didn't cheat his concentration was too focused to notice the thumping in the corridor outside, the muted voices and the sounds of complaint. Before the game was out there was a knock at the door and the woman put the cards down on the table.

'I know exactly where everything is,' she said as she went to the door. 'Don't you dare try to move a thing.'

First into the hallway was a man in his early forties with closely-cropped thinning hair. Whatever business he was in, Bob guessed he was either a director or partner: a boy scout if ever he saw one.

'We need some beds,' he announced. 'Some silly clot left the door open downstairs. More than a dozen people have got in. Some are terribly ... Oh.'

He had glanced into the room. His arrival had woken everyone up.

'Afternoon,' Bob offered.

'Want a hand?' Pushing his middle fingers against the corners of his eyes and up on to the bridge of his nose, Alan rose to his feet.

'Where did you come from?'

'The sewers. We were stuck in there till it rained.' Already the story was beginning to have the ring of a social reminiscence.

'So I can smell. Shouldn't we get you out of your clothes?'

Apart from an absence of glasses, the second man through the door looked much like the first. Peering round his companion he asked more in lip movement than words: 'All right if we come in?'

The first of the injured was the only one conscious, though he barely showed it in the deathly expression on the parts of his face that hadn't peeled away. As he was carried in Bob felt immediately queasy and turned to stare at a picture of gondolas making their way through Venetian mist. Behind him he heard the body being laid on the sofa he had just vacated, and he kept thinking of Venice as another two were brought in, Alan going ahead of them to wake Beat and offer them the double bed.

Sounds of activity began, of water being brought and material being torn, when the first boy scout announced: 'Not much we can do. Just, er, you know, keep them comfortable.' He clearly wasn't too comfortable himself. 'Tell you what, I've got some brandy upstairs. Might help. Why don't you two come with me, get a change of clothes?'

'Great.' Bob welcomed the opportunity to escape. 'I wouldn't like the Queen to catch me in this garb when she comes to inspect the ruins.'

'I'm not sure I've got anything to fit, though. That chap's more my size.'

'That's all right,' said Bob. 'We're not proud.'

John, however, looked as if he was. But when the man insisted, he didn't protest. Speechlessly, he followed them up to the floor above, to a flat identical in layout to the woman's, and the two of them were left in the bedroom to go through the wardrobe. They spoke in whispers so as not to disturb whoever it was asleep in the bed.

'You going to hang on here, or what?' Bob held up a Japanese silk waistcoat several sizes too small. 'Fetching, isn't it?'

'No, it's stopped raining now, I can walk it home from here in half an hour.' John was pulling on a pair of tennis shoes as if to prove the point.

When John didn't ask after his own plans, Bob offered: 'I had thought of stopping with the lady downstairs, but it's getting a bit crowded. Suppose I'd better sod off, too. Where's the best bet?'

John didn't answer for a minute, tying his laces, and if Bob hadn't worked up some respect for the strangely insular, bearded General, the lack of an immediate answer might have got on his nerves. 'It's going to be hard in the town and it's going to be hard in the country.' He said helpfully, 'I suppose, if the woman's right, that there's only been one hit in the south, and with the winds blowing east, then any big town thirty miles or so outside London might be all right.'

'Like what?'

'Reading?'

'What, down the M4?'

'Maybe, but they've probably commandeered all the motorways.'

Somehow Reading seemed like a very long way away but Bob had no other plans. 'Mind if I tag along as far as Hammersmith?'

This time, in the pause before John said 'Okay', Bob knew what he was thinking, that he would rather have been alone. Anti-social bleeder, he thought, and clapped him round the shoulders. 'It always gets me like this. One night with someone and I'll follow them anywhere.' Then he twitched his nose and chuckled to see John wince.

They went back down the stairs, John in a Rex Harrison cardigan turned up at the cuffs, Bob in braces to support trousers with flies that refused to fasten and a navy jersey so expanded over his chest and stomach it looked as if it had been knitted on outsize needles. Neither of them had mentioned Alan and Beat, presuming the couple would have plans of their own, but there they were, hovering by the woman's doorway and Alan immediately wanted to know what their next move was to be. Bob took the opportunity to duck in through the door, saying, 'Won't be a jiff.'

By the sofa the woman was pulling a sheet up over the patient, over the wounds that were now washed and bandaged though they still showed patches of red. On the floor was a bowl Bob knew he shouldn't so much as glance at. Together with the smell of disinfectant and disease was the smell of vomit which by some miracle wasn't his own. He watched the sheet being drawn upwards, relieved that it stopped before it covered the face. There was no point in saying he hadn't the stomach to stay and help.

'Just wanted to say thanks. And, er, I was wondering ...' Wisps of grey eyebrows furrowed over the woman's nose as if she were expecting the worst. 'I was wondering if you had a pack of cards I could buy off you.'

'How much?'

'House in Bow?'

She glanced at the cards still laid out on the table. 'You can't lose something twice, you know – if that's any consolation.'

Bob chuckled. 'Not much.'

From a drawer beneath the table she took out a pack, still in its cellophane. Giving it to him she said: 'Next time round it's double or quits.'

Bob grinned. 'You'll be all right here.'

'Of course I will. Now bugger off.'

With some reluctance Bob obliged. Outside in the corridor John's voice rose from where the three were huddled, still touched by the affinity of the night in the sewer. From among them John's voice came, straining with patience, the real boy-scout leader.

'... all right, stay here, then. All I was saying is that with the top two storeys wiped off this building there's going to be some radiation in the air. I don't know what kind of device has gone off, what its kilotonnage was or anything. Even if we did know, even if we were scientists – look, only last week a group of them were saying there's an error in the recognised lethal dose.' Alan frowned at him as if he were holding something back and Bob thought John would finally lose his cool. Instead he went on: 'There are people who have died of cancer from radiation after working in luminous watch factories and there are people still alive in Hiroshima who were less than half a mile from the epicentre when Big Boy exploded. I don't fucking know what's out there. I just want to get home.'

He turned and stalked down the corridor, unaware that his outburst had impressed them all. Bob pushed past the couple in pursuit, saying quietly as he did so: 'He's lovely when he's roused.' But Beat's scowl told him to leave the man alone. Nevertheless, half-way down the stairs Bob heard footsteps behind him. Though they didn't know what they were letting themselves in for, Beat and Alan were coming too.

Deep pungent breath followed deep pungent breath and the nauseous air of sick and stagnant humanity sunk lower and lower into Tel's lungs. Eyes closed, his head was bent forwards and his hands pressed to his ears to contain a continuing giddiness, but still the cries of the children, the tears and complaints of the adults, got through. Among a forest of legs that supported some kind of life, he remembered he was in the lobby of the Hyde Park Hotel. None of those who pressed at his side offered help: they all had their own problems to attend to. After a while the weakness began to abate and he eased himself unsteadily up to his feet. Though it hardly seemed possible, there were even more people there now, sardine tight, and at the door dozens more were pressing to get in.

'All right now?' It was the lad with the injured arm.

'Fit as a parrot. How long have I been out?'

'I haven't been counting.'

On the stairs the tableau of misery hadn't changed. The same woman sat by the bannisters with a lifeless child in her arms; the same man, his head grotesque and burnt deep black, sat beside her. Nothing had moved except for one man fighting his way towards the stairs who was now being forcibly held back. Tel couldn't bring the girl in here. Careful of wounds and with constant 'excuse me's, he made his way lamely back to the door he had so angrily come in. Outside, the rain had stopped. The commissionaire was still at the top of the steps and so was the sergeant, only now two other uniformed policemen had arrived to spread the word, to urge people to look for shelter, to say that help was on its way. For nearly twenty-four hours the story had been the same.

'What time's this help coming, then?' somebody asked.

'You go and find yourself a room to sit tight in. It'll come.'

'Can't you use your walkie-talkie? Ask when they're getting here?'

'They aren't working, love.'

Catching the sergeant's eye, Tel went up to him. 'It's horrible in there. Nobody's going to get to see that doctor this side of Christmas.'

'Everyone's in the same boat, son.'

'Look, say I'm a tourist. I don't know London. Say I've got a pregnant lady in Hyde Park, just, you know, theoretically, and – theoretically – I ask you where the nearest hospital is.'

The sergeant looked out across the street as if he had chosen to ignore him. When he spoke his voice was only just loud enough for Tel to hear: 'I'd say go straight along to the end of the park, far as you can, then turn on to the road – Kensington High Street – and keep going. Just over a mile on your right's the West London Hospital. Hammersmith.' He turned to look at Tel. 'They've got quite a go-ahead maternity unit there, as I understand it ...'

Tel was off, down the rubble steps and into the growing life of the street. Knightsbridge was different now as people crawled out, peered out, ran out of their hiding places. It was hard to imagine how so many had been concealed, hard to describe the individual anguish, hard to know what they might all do. There was some help for the needy, some self-help for the greedy. There was the law struggling to assert itself, pairs of policemen whose uniform attracted people like honey gets bees. Everyone wanted help, everyone wanted information. In the shove and the shout around the Sheraton Hotel the growing hysteria of voices suddenly pinnacled in a single scream and Tel saw a truncheon raised above the crowd, swing down, come up, swing down again.

Scared for himself, for the girl, for what was left of the world, Tel took to his heels. He was going against the flow, against the exodus of people who were ignoring the warnings about staying under cover. There was little cover left. Tel remembered the underground and its shrill claustrophobia and knew that whatever was in the air it was preferable to such a clawing, living death. His running figure, a vision of fitness that did not describe the body that felt as heavy as lead, attracted attention and, with guilt as his backpack, he ran the gauntlet of cries for help. He leapt the fence into the park, stormed the embankment and slowed down. The girl was still there in the back of the car. He shook his head to toss the beads of sweat from under his hair, opened the door and looked in.

'There's a hospital just up the road.'

It didn't seem to register. Her pale face had a little more colour in it, a slight brownness, like barely-done toast.

'Come on, we've got to give it a go.'

'I'm all right here.'

Tel sighed. He didn't know how long ago it had stopped raining, how many people had passed them by in the night.

Many of them would be heading west, and most would notice any hospital they passed en route. 'I'll give you a piggyback.'

She didn't move but she didn't protest either as Tel guided her from the back seat and hoisted her up on to his back. It was heavy going. Head bent in concentration he watched her red shoes that danced at his knees like a memory of opportunities lost, while his own strange dark brogues pushed on, willed forwards under the weight. There was no diverting his gaze at the sites that he knew lay around them, until the girl spoke.

'There's so little left.'

'There's got to be something ... somewhere.' His words came out between each dull breath. 'Back by the car there was a patch of daffodils. Still blooming. They looked great. When we've got you sorted out we could head for the country. There's got to be something there. A bit of land. We could ... I mean, you know, if you wanted ...'

He swallowed hard, caught both by a sudden thought that he was being presumptuous and by a stabbing pain in the chest. He wasn't going to be able to take her all the way. By the second set of lights, at the end of South Carriage Drive, he set her down on her feet and they stood for a moment in silence.

'I'll try the cars again.'

As at Albert Gate they were piled up here and by now no hiding place remained unexplored. Doors were open, glove compartments rifled, boots and bonnets yawning into the air. Still he went among them like an old hand, a connoisseur with an eye for a bargain. Until he found it he hadn't known what he was looking for. When he came across it, overlooked in the back of a large estate, he couldn't help being surprised at his good luck – the punter at the village fete who'd spotted the Constable. He pulled out the collapsible bicycle, opened it up and secured it into its proper shape. The sight of it even made the girl feel better.

'Hop on and I'll give you a push.'

And they were off, into Kensington Gardens, past the ruin of the Albert Memorial, the girl clinging tight, Tel holding the saddle and guiding her along singing 'Raindrops Keep Falling on my Head'.

'Are you a good farmer?' she asked.

'Me? I'm the Walter Gabriel of West Ham.'

'What are those flowers, then?'

Ahead of them, to the right, were patches of blooms, yellow and white, arrogant in the dust of the burned and grey ground.

'Them? Er, well, they're not daffodils.'

'No.'

'They're the other ones.'

She laughed. 'I'll look after the garden. You can take care of the animals.'

Despite the throwing together, the confessions of the night and the kiss of the morning, up until now Tel hadn't been sure. Now he knew, he knew he'd done well for himself. He broke into a trot and tried not to sound too over-the-moon. 'That's all right by me. At least I can tell a sheep from a cow.'

'What's the difference?'

'Everyone knows that. Neither of them bark and they both give milk.'

'Suddenly I get the feeling that from now on nothing in this life is going to be easy.'

Nor was it. At the end of the park they ran out of pathway and turned into Kensington High Street where the scene was as bad as Knightsbridge had been. Some of the cars had tried to escape along pavements where building had buried them; a bus, on its side, was right across the road. Only feet were equipped to get through. His arm about her, Tel supported the girl on the hour-long slog towards the West London Hospital that was little more than a mile away. They kept their heads low, avoiding the cries, watching their footfalls, skirting the debris and the occasional corpse and limb that poked through. But Tel had an eye open for police and apparent officials who stood in the human tide and attempted to stem its flow. Some of those they stopped sat down where they were, others argued, others did as they were told. Bit by bit the crowd was being filtered, thinned out, turned away. They passed over the railway bridge into Hammersmith Road where the glass domes of Olympia were now nothing but scorched iron girders. Here the group of officials was no small patrol; it was a solid pack. Tel looked determinedly away from them and steered the girl over rubble on the other side of the road.

'Where do you think you're going?' The voice was sharp in the eerie quiet of the street.

'To the hospital. She's sick.'

'You're not going anywhere. Get in that building.'

'Piss off.'

None of the three who were suddenly at his side wore uniforms but their sheer bulk carried the unmistakable weight of the law. There was no argument. They went quietly, herded into the exhibition hall that had only half a roof. It was the same sick place as the hotel had been, stretching out on all sides, and Tel felt the girl shudder beneath his grasp.

'We can't stay here,' she whispered.

'Let's move round, see if we can find another way out.'

The place was enormous, the people camped on the exhibitors' stands and across the aisles, taking up space with small piles of personal belongings. There were mattresses, too, and makeshift beds. Some of the inmates must have been there since the whole thing began. It took them a while to make their way to the back of the place, around stands of computer equipment, past the part where the sky opened up, and down a side passage to a door marked 'Emergency Exit'. Tel pushed the bar gratefully back. And half a dozen men outside, some armed, turned to see them.

'Shut it.'

Tel hesitated for a moment, but again there was little choice.

'Buggers won't even let you die in peace.'

Tel glanced at the young man who had spoken. He was smiling like an idiot, as if he was a good friend. 'We'd have been better off in the park.'

'Hello!' The girl saw it first but it wasn't until Tel noticed the T-shirt that he let himself smile, too. 'Shit, it's you.'

'Glad you're all right anyway. Come on, you can't get out of here, we've checked all the doors. They've got us walled up. I've got some mates and there's a bit to drink. You look like you need it.'

An acquaintance of no more than a day was an old friend, a

small compensation for not being able to get out. He strode confidently ahead of them and Tel remembered the way he and his companion had leapt across the cars. The girl must have remembered it, too.

'Is Marvin here?' she asked.

He shook his head. 'They got him.'

'Where is he?' Tel asked.

'Dead. He nicked some milk for a geezer we found who was a bit thirsty. He didn't stop when the Old Bill asked him to, so they shot him up.'

The sounds were the clue to the activity going on around King's Road: the shouts of the rescuers, the groans of the rescued, the wails of the abandoned, the crash of the rubble, the scrape of the shovels, the pounding of mechanical diggers now trying to clear the streets. Occasionally, too, came explosions from something ignited in distant fires. Sensing possibilities in the air, Bob was whistling distractedly, trilling unconnected notes, as he strode alongside Beat and Alan, pursuing the furtive, wiry figure of John. Before they had left the block of flats, John had warned them to look out for officials, had said they might be armed and would not hesitate to shoot if people did not do as they were told. It was hard to know if, in his anger, he hadn't been exaggerating, and his decision to reach Hammersmith by the back streets wasn't a deliberate obstacle race, a penalty for their wanting to tag along.

'Look out!' Beat grabbed at Bob's jersey, tugging him back. An estate car shot past, moving along a lane cleared in King's Road.

Bob chuckled. 'That would have been a bit ironic, wouldn't it?' As they crossed and continued up the road ahead of them, he asked: 'Where are you two off to, then?'

'Beat's brother's got a farm in Dorset.' Alan had stepped to one side to let through two men carrying a lifeless body. 'We're going to try to get down there.'

'Nice, Dorset, is it?'

Beat laughed. '*Wonderful*. What about you?'

'Reading,' he said automatically. Then: 'To be honest, I

don't fancy going anywhere. A nice little flat like that old lady's would suit me fine. With a nice little old lady to look after me, too.'

He pressed his hands into his trouser pockets, one touching the bank notes, the other the cards. It didn't look as if it was going to be that easy to find a poker school. Suddenly he caught a whiff of something cooking and his stomach, long neglected by a proper meal, gave a lurch.

Beat caught it, too. 'What's that smell?'

'High tea?' Bob suggested.

'It's high all right.'

'Tut, who's choosey?'

But it wasn't tea that was cooking, it was human flesh. At the top of the street, on the grey grass beside St Luke's church, a great pyre was crackling, fuelled by cans of petrol sucked from cars. Tending it were two policemen, not armed as John had suggested, nor apparently interested in anyone around them apart from a small band of helpers led by a vicar who was too busy to kneel and pray. A quick feel for a pulse on the wrists by the policemen was all the confirmation they needed to ensure the victims were dead. Personal documents were removed for identification of the bodies which were then, with as much dignity as such a ceremony could afford, heaped on to the pile.

'John!' Alan's call stopped him and he waited for them to catch up. 'Can't we do anything. Shouldn't we ...'

'What?' John was sharp.

'Perhaps we could help bring in some of the dead.'

'You'd be here for a week. Look, we're better off than most. We missed the early fallout, there's a chance we'll live.'

'A *chance*?'

'Yes, a chance. We're not even four miles from the blast. Yes, all right, burning some bodies might help, but the disease that's going to come in the next couple of weeks is going to need more than a few bonfires to stop. That's just a bit of religious voodoo going on over there, that's all.'

As he stalked off again, the others meekly following behind, Bob wondered how John would have behaved if, like himself, his family had been wiped out in the first explosion, if getting home wasn't now too much of an excuse and that he was, wife and children aside, as selfish as sin. Perhaps it was that same selfish streak which had kept them all alive until now. He would never know. They crossed Sydney Street, John looking to left and right not for traffic but for armed men he imagined would be lurking, then turned down another side road.

At first, when Bob glanced down the next turning on the right, he didn't realise it was him. His balding head glowing red, his shirt in tatters and a scarlet gash across his right shoulder, he was struggling with a timber that poked from the front-room window of a half-collapsed house. Only when he looked away did it register and he looked back again. The man was in trouble. There was no one else visible in the cul-de-sac and the piece of wood the man was battling with was several times his size. When Bob turned to tell the others, Alan was staring over his shoulder. Bob made a gesture, about to say something, but Alan turned away, put his arm around Beat and hurried her on. Bob was in no doubt that Alan, too, had recognised Jeffrey Bishop.

Alerted by the footfalls, Bishop looked up to see Bob approach. 'What are you doing here?'

'Thought we'd have a reunion of the Grand Order of Sewer Rats. What's the problem?'

'There's a girl in there, a young teenager. She's trapped. Hold on to this.'

The beam lodged on Bob's shoulder, cutting into the corner of his neck, and Bishop disappeared back in through the open front door. For nearly ten minutes Bob took the weight, his face growing red, his legs sometimes near to shaking with the effort. When Bishop did finally emerge he wasn't carrying the girl but two lengths of four-by-two.

'I need a hand,' he said. 'We'll have to prop the beam up. Here.'

One piece was shorter than the other and it took him a few minutes to pile rubber up around it before Bob could slip out from under the beam. He gripped his sore shoulder and made windmill motions with his arm.

'That going to be all right?'

'Should be, as long as there's vertical pressure on it. Come on.'

Inside the front room the girl lay half-buried in the mess that was once the ceiling, her fresh face brushed with plaster and chunks of it like monster dandruff in her scattered long blonde hair. The beam that came in through the window angled down along the length of her body, about a foot above it. Another was still pinned horizontally across her chest. She had a bearing about her which the disaster hadn't taken away. A nice kid, Bob thought, and he was immediately conscious of the pale blue Marks and Spencer briefs showing behind his unzippable fly.

'Hello,' he said, trying to be cheery. "Scuse my clothes. I couldn't find a phone box. You probably didn't recognise me without my cape.'

Her eyes remained distant, so hungry for help, and her whole face said simply: 'It hurts.' The jokes would have to come later. He went to help Bishop, the two of them carefully levering up the beam that straddled her chest. When it began to shift, the girl closed her eyes and took in a breath, a pleasure that brought an almost immediate contortion of pain when her lungs caught on the crushed ribs.

'Can you move?' Bishop asked, and when she didn't answer he said to Bob: 'We've got to drag her out of here. Can you hold this by yourself for about twenty seconds?'

'No idea, but I'll have a go.'

Bishop let go and moved towards the girl. It wasn't the timber that Bob was holding which let them down. In their movement, in disturbing the debris, the pressure on the beam that stretched out through the window and into the road had shifted. The props outside gave way, the beam collapsed and more of the ceiling fell in with it. Bob could hold on no longer. The timber slipped from his shoulder, forcing him backwards. Beneath its weight, Bob's legs and Bishop's back were crushed.

14: MANOEUVRES

According to the lieutenant, the task force he would be taking into Durham would consist of only half a dozen soldiers. There was no fire-fighting equipment to spare and no ordnance supplies, but there was a chance he might be able to take some equipment from the town - picks, shovels, wheelbarrows, buckets, blankets. The doctor had explained which were the most important medical supplies and how they should be distributed. After some debate, the council had agreed to part with a water lorry. Two open trucks, going round the town like rag-and-bone carts, had rounded up all the households had to offer and taken the plunder up to the Trading Estate to be sorted out, together with fruit, sliced bread, tinned goods and just a sample from no less than three lorries which had turned up with pork scratchings. Least successful had been the response to the request for fire-fighting equipment which had almost entirely been used up on the fires that had broken out just after the blast.

In the end, however, the lieutenant never arrived. Instead, a small TAVR detail came up from Bishop Auckland with no explanation for the change of plan and the news that there was to be no expedition into the city. The disappointment everyone felt was not confined to the town. All day the students who continued to ferry the injured out of the city had been waiting for the lieutenant and his convoy to bring relief to those who were desperate for it. So many of the citizens had remained in Durham when they, too, could have left, preferring to spend what might be the last of their energy digging the victims out of the rubble, comforting those who could not be moved and taking those who could over the brick-and-mortar hillocks to the edges of the devastation where cars might take them away. After the initial tide of evacuees the number of cars reaching Spennymoor had been reduced to no more than two or three an hour.

With the rescuers came continuing tales of the appalling disaster. Not a single road in the city was passable. The

Newcastle Road which had vaporised in the crater of Pity Me had also collapsed on to the railway line on the west side of town. The roads to the east, to the motorway, were strewn with debris and burned-out cars and only bulldozers, which would not arrive for many days, could clear them away. The massive stones from the cathedral's west towers had dammed the river and the stagnant water was littered with bodies. The whole of the peninsular which for centuries had stood firm against the Scots was completely unassailable and it would be weeks before anyone could be found among the steep slopes of the old town. All over the city there were messages daubed on stones like callers' slates on cottages in the old mining towns: 'John, gone to look for Peter. Be back when it gets dark.' 'I'm alive! – Pauline Gibbons', 'Dierdre, where are you?' And among the tales one stood out, haunting all those who had passed by Old Elvet. There the fifteen-foot high walls had caved in on Durham Prison, the roofs collapsed and the ancient oak-timbered buildings that formed part of the complex had poured their fire across all that remained, scorching the gates with their blue plaque which threatened five years' imprisonment to anyone attempting to help a prisoner to escape. Not one of the 850 inmates had come out alive.

In the middle of the afternoon, Maggie Blackett brought news of another, much greater threat. Ted Evans was in the process of trying to sort out a better way of dealing with the flood of requests for news of friends and relatives. The old town hall, assigned to the task, was filling too fast.

'They've found it,' she announced as she came into the room.

'Found what?'

'The missile. I've just been talking to a student who's come from the town. It's buried in the playing fields up by the observatory.'

'Oh no!' Everyone stopped dead. It was closer, on this side of the city.

'I've told the army. They're going to send a special unit up here as soon as they can. They'll have to come this way. The TAs are clearing a space for them to get through up at the roundabout and I've organised with the depot for a couple of bulldozers to go with them. They'll be needed to get that far into the city.'

'We must evacuate.' The thought of the whole town, together with more than a thousand dying patients just getting up and going was a daunting one.

'The army won't let us. We have to stay here until they've checked out the device.'

'If this gets out the whole town will panic.'

'They're sending more TAs up from Bishop to make sure we stay where we are.'

'Nice of them to tell us.'

Maggie shrugged, then she left to go and wait for the unit to arrive. For half an hour she paced up and down inside the working men's club, a modern square block near the roundabout on the edge of the Bessemer Estate. All its bottles, its cans and its kegs had already been distributed. Now it was stacked with boxes and crates brought across from the Trading Estate waiting for the next round of handouts. When the army unit eventually turned up, it came not as a khaki convoy but in two commandeered police Range Rovers with half a dozen soldiers and equipment. As they came to a halt at the roundabout they put on the masks of their 'Noddy' suits and a major, who had removed his flat hat to put on the breathing gear, stepped out as if he were coming to visit the victims of the bubonic plague. When he reached the club, however, he took the mask off again, to show a face that could not conceal some anxiety. He introduced himself to Maggie and took from the map pocket in his trousers an Ordnance Survey of the area, folded over so that she could not see all the marks that were drawn on it. But she could see the red cross at Pity Me and another a millimetre to the west of the red dot of the station at Chester-le-Street. She pointed out the observatory just beyond Elvet Hill.

'Where's the chap who found it?'

'He went back into the city. I couldn't stop him. There are lots of students running the taxi service back and forth. We, of course, aren't allowed to go in ourselves, or send in any help.' There was a slight note of disdain in her voice which was not lost on the major.

'I understand how you feel. But we have tremendous

problems at the moment. Tremendous. We're fully stretched. There isn't one ounce of help that isn't going somewhere.'

She nodded. 'I don't know if anybody has mentioned it but we have two bulldozers here which you will need to get through to the observatory. Do you have anybody who can drive them?'

'Yes. How will we find the exact spot?'

'The student said he would be at the observatory and he says there are two policemen guarding it. You, er, you couldn't take a water lorry in with you, could you? It's just that they're expecting something in the city. We were told a reconnaissance party was going to go in this afternoon and they'll be very disappointed when you turn up, empty handed.'

He looked doubtful. 'Can you spare the water?'

'Of course not, but their need is marginally greater than ours.'

'All right, just one lorry.'

She smiled her thanks but already the major's thoughts seemed to be elsewhere.

'How safe is the warhead?' she asked.

'If it hasn't gone off so far, about ninety-nine point nine per cent.'

He put on his mask and she followed him out of the building to make sure the bulldozers and water lorry joined the convoy before it set off. Then she got in her car and set off to find the doctor in the health centre. She had not gone far, however, when one of the newly-arrived Territorial Army soldiers stepped out in front of her, the fingers of his right hand by the guard of an old Lee Enfield, to force the car to stop. When she explained who she was, it wasn't enough. He wanted to see her papers.

'What sort of papers?' she demanded.

All the paper she had in her handbag – driving licence, blood-donor card, library ticket, letters addressed to her – weren't enough and the soldier insisted on accompanying her to the council offices so that she could verify who she was.

Inside the car, he said: 'I gather we've got one of you locked up already.'

'Yes. For the crime of wanting to know what was going on.'

'There's the radio, what's wrong with that?'

'I don't know, soldier.' She banged the buttons on the car radio with an angry fist. 'Just what *is* wrong with it?'

'Ah, well, that will be the effect of what we call the radio flash, you see ...'

Outside the council offices Maggie was startled to see that the TAVR had pitched a tent. It was here, after checking with the chief executive that she was who she said she was, that she was issued with 'papers', a printed slip torn from a pad that looked like the ones British Rail issued to people caught without a proper ticket. With that stuck to the windscreen with sticky tape she went back through the town to the health centre.

There was no sign of Dr MacGilvray there, so she braced herself to go over to the sports centre. The stench of it reached her long before she got to the doors. Inside, however, there was some order coming in to the chaos. On the wood block floors mattresses were in neat rows, the patients all covered and the helpers numerous. She caught MacGilvray's red-rimmed eye and he came over to see her. The young locum was with him.

'It's time you had some sleep, Doctor,' she said. 'You won't be doing anybody any good if you get too tired.'

'I know. We've a rota going. It's this young man's turn next, then I'll take my turn.'

'Is there anything more I can do?'

'Put the clock back.' He rubbed his eyes with the heel of his hand. 'I don't suppose the blood transfusion unit came up with the army?'

'No. You heard about the bomb, then?'

'Yes, it's all we need. I'm surprised we haven't had any more coronary patients.'

'Look at it this way, doctor.' She smiled broadly. 'It's got the road cleared between here and Durham.'

'That's all very well, but who's going to take any help in?'

'There's nothing to stop the students going back to the city with a lorry instead of a car.'

Two hours later, however, when the army unit returned, Maggie Blackett faced a heavy grilling that left no room for smiles. There had been no warhead, no police, no student. After spending all that time beating a path into the city, nobody they had spoken to had known what on earth they were talking about.

15: HAMMERSMITH

At first Shirley had refused to go downstairs, back into the cellar Jack had declared free from rats. Not only had he killed both of the vermin, he said, but three more he had found in the kitchen. The doors were now securely shut against further intrusion and a thorough search of the house had revealed no more of them. But dust might still be coming into the house and, as the radio continued to urge, people were still best off hiding. The vigorous shaking of her head had turned him away and he had left the bathroom to stomp round the house looking for things to take down to the cellar. By the end of the afternoon, on his third visit to persuade her to leave, he told her it was comfortable down there, homely almost, with the Primus and the lamp he had found now working, a chair from the sitting room he had taken the cover from, and two mattresses from the children's room making half-way decent beds. From among blankets and clothes he had collected from dust-free wardrobes and drawers he had also found an old jersey and a pair of corduroy trousers of John's to wear.

Finally, by way of an ultimatum, he picked the boy up and carried him from the bathroom. There was no alternative. A few minutes later Shirley followed them down the stairs, her shoulders hunched and her stomach churning as if she were walking along the edge of Beachy Head. The cellar had, indeed, improved, the turmoil become order – the chair, the mattresses, the blankets, a clutter of artefacts that tried to be inviting. Yet the invitation was still to a bleak room of grey walls and concrete floor and the little touches seemed almost desperate, like pin-ups in a prisoner's cell. There was a smell, too, which had not gone away, an airlessness of a place occupied for a long time, more pungent than a car after a long journey and, with it, the odour of the terrors the cold-hearted chamber had seen. In the middle of it Jack began cracking new-found eggs into a pan on the blue-flaming Primus, helped by Simon who had not eaten since the interrupted breakfast earlier that day.

Shirley curled up on one of the mattresses, her eyes never still, flickering, roaming, penetrating the gloom, unable to believe her nightmare had gone away. Sometimes her eyes would catch Jack's which would be curious and thoughtful but she would not hold his gaze and would look quickly away. He and Simon were getting on well, the boy fetching things, holding things, doing as the man asked in a voice that growled without harshness or threat. Shirley accepted the plate of eggs Simon finally brought her but she had no appetite for them, picking at the corners and poking at the yolks until their oozing amber flowed to remind her of the soft cheek she had punctured the night before. Her refusal to eat the meal Simon had helped to prepare upset the boy and he became demanding, wanting to know why she wouldn't eat.

'I'm not hungry.'

'But it's special.'

His tantrum flared and he would not eat his own supper until she took him on her lap and spoon-fed him like a baby. It had been a very long day.

'It's nearly time for bed.' It was a guess. She hadn't bothered to look at the clock since she came into the room.

'I don't want to go to bed.'

'You don't need to wash or do your teeth. Come on, lie down and I'll tell you a story.'

'But I don't want to.'

Jack interrupted the clearing away to toss on to the mattress some books he had found in his scavenging. Shirley was grateful for them and she read the familiar tales to the sound of Simon's tongue slapping against his thumb in his mouth. But even after they were finished he fought against sleep and Shirley lay down beside him, pulled the blanket over the two of them and sang quiet lullabies. In a while the warm, milky breaths became slower and Shirley, too, succumbed to drowsiness. It was short-lived. As if a bolt of electricity had shot through her body, she twitched violently and in an instant knew where she was: in a cold sweat, in a cell, on a hard floor, alone. Pushing herself up on one elbow she looked round the room and wondered how she could be so imprisoned here.

'They've all gone,' Jack said flatly. Sitting in the easy chair he was watching her.

'They'll never go. I can't stand it now. What am I going to be like in a few days' time? It's only the thought of Simon and Jenny ...'

He stood up and went to the Primus where a small pan was boiling and tipped the water into a cup. 'Tea?'

'Yes.'

He handed her the cup, then made one for himself, bringing it to the edge of the mattress with a carton of milk and a packet of sugar. After dishing them out he sat down and Shirley stared into her cup, holding it in both hands, as if her future lay there. Then she felt the back of his hand, the coarseness of its skin gently touching her cheek and when she looked up at him his thumb wiped softly over the hollows beneath her eyes where her tears had been. She shivered. It was strange, out of place, yet for the first time since the disaster had come she was aware of real human warmth. With the expression on his face wide open to any interpretation she might care to give it he stood up and walked away, taking his cup and putting it down beside the pail they used as a sink. Then he tugged at the corner of the other mattress and dragged it across the floor to place it next to hers. Lying down he put an arm round her and let her head fall on to his chest. In a while the heavy hand which reached nearly from ear to ear tugged a little at the dry, mousy hair making it tingle at the roots, and when the palm pressed down on her head to stop the tingling it felt like the valve of a pressure cooker being pushed down, containing the anguish, flattening the fears.

It was not quite what she wanted, some ten minutes later, when he raised her head by the chin and pressed his fleshy lips on hers, touching them to her face, to her cheeks, to her ears, to her eyes, to her throat. Yet she knew she could have expected it. With little control over her ragged emotions her whole body responded without warning, coming to life and urging on the violation. In one way it seemed fitting that after her city, her family, her home had been plundered she herself should be next. She desired it, though, too, longed for the stranger who was now caressing, cupping, gorging her breasts, to be safe inside her, engulfing her with the strength and the compassion he had shown in the past day. When it happened, she was released, set loose on a wild plain that stretched way beyond the walls that enclosed her, and as she burst through the surf of her ecstasy she called out the name of the man she had been faithful to all her life.

Afterwards they lay still without speaking and Shirley found further, deeper comfort when she realised she felt no remorse. Dozing quietly, she was alerted to the sound of Jack coughing, a dull rumble that became chesty until the whole mattress shook. Rolling away from her, he stood up, jerking violently as if contorted by puppet strings. When it had passed he breathed in deeply then pulled on his clothes. She watched him without stirring as she might have watched her husband go to the bathroom in the middle of the night. Without glancing back he went up the stairs and into the house where his footsteps trailed over her head towards the front door. He would come back; he had come back before. In the mess of her passion she lay listening until the footfalls returned across the boards above her. It did not occur to her that it might be John coming home.

In a side street that led in to the north end of Fulham Palace Road, John had left Beat and Alan and run off in the opposite direction, pursuing his determined path in the terrace-lined maze which led directly to his own front door. His final instructions were precise: these were the roads to take, avoid all main thoroughfares, wait until dark, smuggle yourselves on any vehicle going out of town. The words were as unemotional as any he had spoken since they had met and Alan saw that the parting, despite their shared ordeal, was no more than another incident to him.

Convinced there must be more to be said, Alan began: 'We must keep in touch. If you're ever in Dorset ...' And it was only after John was a fleeting mountain-goat of a figure that Beat laughed.

'What's so funny?' He felt vulnerable, on edge.

She tucked an arm in his and drew him in the direction they had been ordered. 'You. When you said we must keep in touch. It sounded as if we had met on a holiday.'

'Well, he was a good guide.'

It was the first light moment in the attempted exodus which had been going on for more than two hours through nearly three miles of ruins, where roofs were shattered and windows smashed. The sewer had prepared them for the rats which freely scavenged, but for little else; not for the scale of destruction the damaged acres implied, not for the corpses, the burned and cut bodies, nor for the dispiriting hopelessness brought by the cries of despair. Groups of helpers were more sparse than they had been around Fulham and King's Road and no organised rescue parties had reached into these backroads where most of the residents had battened down. A few still roamed the streets with their grief, with their disbelief, with their open wounds and undisguised pain. As individual insignificance became more apparent, what charity there was was wearing thin. In one street a man staggered from a house with bloody scrapes on his dark lips and cheeks. 'Bastards,' he said to John, 'all I did was ask for some water.' Then he slumped where he stood, his eyes glazing over. They had hurried on.

Now, as the couple crossed Fulham Palace Road they could see no sign of the malevolent armed forces John had warned them against and Alan wondered if John hadn't been reading too many left-wing books. They crossed between the cars and turned down Crisp Road towards the river.

'I wonder if Bob found his nice old lady,' Beat suddenly said.

'Who knows.'

It was a sight he wouldn't forget. Bob's round figure, his quizzical look as he nodded towards the side street and the unexpected figure of Jeffrey Bishop. Alan had not mentioned it to Beat at the time, and he never would. Only circumstance had placed them together, only caution and time could keep them there, and the reappearance of Bishop might have been enough to drive a wedge between them again. Since their conversation the previous night in the sewer he had realised, for the first time and with some alarm, that he was not as intelligent as she was. He had never felt that of a woman before. He wasn't in control, he would just have to let their relationship grow. That was why, in the flat, he had made a point of not sharing the large bed with her, even if they were only going to sleep. 'Up to you,' she had said with what sounded like genuine indifference. It was up to him and he had left her in peace.

In silence they passed by the burned-out Riverside Studios and turned left down towards the walkway along by the river. It was growing dark and the bridge, once cream and golden brown, blazoned with coats of arms, stood blackly against the dusk. On the oposite bank beneath limp-leaved trees, small fires burned, keeping clumps of unseen people warm. The tide was up and the water moved slowly; it was on the turn. But the flotillas of disfigured corpses were out of sight, hidden by the flood-high wall.

'It's going to take years to clear everything up. There will have to be another capital somewhere else.' London was the only place Alan had ever worked and though he had nowhere else but Dorset to go to, he was beginning to realise that it might be a permanent exile. Tomorrow's children would only know about London from history books. 'Imagine a decade's August Bank Holiday crowds all together. That's the kind of influx there's going to be down in the west country. How is anybody ever going to organise them?'

'Anarchy.'

'Absolutely.'

'No, I mean real, political anarchy, where there are just small communities everywhere, each governing themselves.'

Two days ago he would have contradicted her, laughed and told her she was wrong, that anarchy means, as everyone knew, the breakdown of law and order. Today he knew better: he didn't believe her but she might just be right. The conversation was interrupted anyway. They were emerging from the far side of the bridge when two gunshots cracked out over their heads. It stopped them dead. As they stepped back under the bridge, not daring to look, they heard shouts, a fierce argument which was resolved by the rattling volley of some kind of machine-gun. In the clamour that this produced, Alan flapped his hands for Beat to follow him forwards and as they ran he hoped the scuffle would keep everyone on the bridge looking anywhere but down at them. Under the blanketing dusk they could have been hardly more than shadows slipping along the path, turning right and ducking low beside the brick wall of the approach road to the bridge. The muscles in Alan's thighs and calves tightened, begging him not to crouch lower and lower as he ran beside the diminishing wall. When it finally offered no protection at all, he straightened and urged Beat in front of him and they made for the small road up ahead, a cul-de-sac beyond which he could just make out the brooding shape of the flyover. As he followed, not turning to see the fracas, an arc of bullets hammered into a van on his left and it was impossible to tell if they were stray or if somebody was aiming at him. He didn't stop to find out. Reaching the side road he carried on running alongside the cottages until he caught up with Beat at the end of the row. Looking back then, there was no sign of either the bridge or anyone in pursuit.

Together they crouched by the garden fence of the last house, peering out, breathing deeply and not saying a word. Just to the right was the roundabout beneath the flyover which descended in front of them to scoop up the Great West Road a few yards to their left. A single lane of traffic had so far been cleared on the opposite, east-bound exit road which led to Hammersmith Broadway, but the six assorted lorries parked with their lights on at the far side of the roundabout had gone as far as they could. A terrific explosion had caused the British Oxygen Company to vanish, a crater to open up across the road and a vast chunk of the flyover to come crashing down. By a pillar beneath the black fingers of torn reinforced concrete a bonfire glowed brightly and Alan could make out the glinting black metal of the guards' arms and the head-to-toe khaki radiation suits of the drivers. Alan at last began to know the feeling that John had tried to instil in them: as civilians they were enemies in their own town.

'Do you think they'll be going back where they came from?' Beat whispered.

'Bound to be.'

'Couldn't we ask them for a lift?'

'Could do. But if they don't want to give us one, there's no telling what they might have in mind for us.'

After a while, restless from waiting to see what the vehicles would do, Alan excused himself and walked a few yards back down the road. 'Smuggle yourself on any vehicle going out of town,' John had said, and the cold words now chilled him, making him feel like a child, for that was the last time he had known absolute fear. He looked at the black windows of the house whose garden he was now loudly watering. If he just knocked, perhaps someone would let him in. In the distance, however, came the sound of an engine starting up, and it brought him back towards thoughts of Dorset and the original plan.

Settling himself down, with a tight grin, beside Beat again, he saw that the unloading was over and the last lorry in the queue, the one nearest to them, had begun to reverse down the road. Then it turned, anti-clockwise, into the roundabout where a gap in the traffic gave it room to manoeuvre, and it swung back, bumping one or two cars out of the way. The gears crashed and it moved forwards again, turning west and speeding off towards the M4. Then the next, a Luton, began the same routine.

'Fourth one,' Alan whispered shakily. 'That's the only one that hasn't got a solid body. Let's go over there, to where they're backing up. The driver won't see us if we stand right behind him – nor should the guards. We'll have to be quick.' When Beat said nothing he asked: 'Got any better ideas?'

'Not one.'

As soon as the third lorry was on its way, Alan took Beat's hand and they scuttled over the road to the roundabout. Crouching beside a car at the back of the gap, they watched the dropside-and-tilt Bedford reverse towards them, its back lights glowing red. Alan stood up and pushed Beat forwards. The brake lights lit their faces. He called: 'Jump!'

Grabbing her hips he heaved her up the tailboard until her head disappeared between the tarpaulin flaps. Her legs see-sawed upwards, showing the mauve-tinted cuts Alan had all but forgotten about. Then the brake lights went out, the gear lever slipped home and he lunged for the top of the tailboard. In horror he felt the lorry kangaroo backwards towards the car behind. His legs flailed wildly and by some miracle were out of the way of the lorry and the car when they crashed. Then he hauled himself through the flaps and tipped down into the pitch darkness, landing on his hands and knees. The lorry lurched forwards and he fell against something soft.

'Ouch.'

'Sorry.' Sitting down next to her he shivered as all the fear drained out of him. Then he listened for a while as something unseen – a jack or a toolbox – clattered on the metal floor.

'God,' he said finally, 'it's wonderful to be moving.'

That wasn't the only reason he was beginning to feel better. They had boarded the lorry safely and, with luck, were heading away from the danger, away from the poisonous air and the city in its death throes. And it was he alone who had ensured this last part of their escape. With the thought of success, some self-respect returned and he risked putting an arm round Beat. Her head fell easily on to his shoulder and a warmness something like pleasure bristled at the back of his neck.

'Do you think you can sleep?' he asked.

'Forever.'

There was no telling how long they had. It would have been too much to hope that they would nod off now and wake up in Bristol where no one was injured, where there was food in the shops, drink in the pubs, and hot baths ran all night. Though it was only two hours down the motorway, the thought of walking through a normal, functioning city seemed to Alan as remote as World War Three had been two days ago. In a few minutes Beat suddenly felt heavier and he knew she had managed to fall asleep. In spite of his own aching tiredness, he stayed awake, thinking very little as the miles rattled past, glimpsing the red-glow of London's still-burning skyline each time the tarpaulin flapped open.

In less than half an hour, they lurched to the left, taking a corner too tightly to be on the motorway. Fifteen minutes and more corners later they came to a stop. Anxiously, Alan heard voices outside and the hum of a generator. Light, actual man-made light, unseen for so long, peeked into the cracks around the tarpaulin. To wake Beat, Alan kissed her on the forehead. It had no effect, so he moved his arm away and said: 'We're here.'

'Where?' she said in a sigh.

'Not too far away. About twenty miles from London, I'd guess.' He was whispering, not wanting those outside the lorry to hear. But before he had a chance to work out how they would now escape, the tarpaulin flaps were thrown back and they were blinded by the light of the headlamps on a lorry parked behind. The stocky, middle-aged man dressed in overalls who pulled down the tailboard and jumped inside saw them at once.

''Ello, a couple of stowaways. You all right?'

'Fine,' Alan said guardedly. 'Where are we?'

'Heathrow cargo. Where did you get on?'

'Hammersmith.'

'Well, you'd better hop off again – unless you want to go back to the old smoke. We're loading up for the return trip.' He caught a parcel thrown up to him and put it down at the front of the lorry. As he stowed it, Alan noticed the label on its side: 'Oxfam/Ethiopia: Medical supplies. Handle with care.'

The man saw him looking.

'Yeah, we've had to divert some of the stuff in the warehouses. They aren't flying any more supplies in tonight. Too dangerous.'

They walked to the back of the truck together and Alan helped Beat climb down. Above them the man shouted out to the darkness: 'Bernie!'

'What?'

'You going over to the terminals?'

'That I am.'

'There's couple here need a lift.'

'Right-o.'

The man continued stacking the parcels while the spectre of the radiation-suited driver appeared in the headlights. His mask was off now, showing a face around the same age as the man in overalls, with eyes sunk in tiredness and perspiration on his forehead which he wiped incautiously with his sleeve.

'You were lucky,' he grinned. 'There's a lot of law up there with guns. They're getting a bit shirty with people who won't stay put. There's some around here, too, so you better stay close with one of us, otherwise they might think you're an illegal immigrant or something and open up. Bernie?'

'Coming.'

'These two are okay for Terminal 3.'

'What happens in Terminal 3?' Beat asked.

'Intercontinental. That's where the lucky ones like you go. If you're sick you get sent off to European, Terminal 2.'

'And Terminal 1?'

'British Airways and domestic. It's fucking diabolical. There's thousands of them just dying in there.'

None of the supplies unloaded at Hammersmith flyover reached the sick at Olympia less than one mile away. Between them were the old West London and the Charing Cross hospitals and their beds had already been full when the alarm was raised. After the explosion the injured who had been caught beneath the Cunard Hotel and the mirror-glass façades of the brand new office complex at Hammersmith Broadway had been among the first to seek help from the hospitals. Later, other injured and sick, knowing them to be nearby, had made their way there from where they had been hidden – in the underground, the borough library, the Palais. At Charing Cross doctors and nurses had been among the many casualties when the three fourteen-storey east-facing sides of the X-shaped building shattered their panes. At the West London, fractured gas pipes had caused the boilers in the basement to explode and an initial attempt to evacuate the building in which alarming cracks had appeared had been abandoned under the weight of the constantly-arriving patients – not least of all the newborn in the hospital's maternity wards.

In the six hours since the lane in the Great West Road and M4 had been cleared, supplies to the hospitals had been dribbling in. With them came the news of the country outside, together with instructions on policing, suggestions of self-help and, from the highest authorities, the order that everyone must, for the moment, stay where they were. The group beneath the flyover – mostly policemen, but also Territorials who had been unable to receive any messages of call-up, and several officials from the Town Hall – now formed part of a cordon which was being gradually wrapped around the city. Within this outer cordon, to lessen its burden, were inner cordons, some merely barriers in arbitrary streets, some encircling whole buildings, like the halls at Olympia.

In the Grand Hall many had managed to escape the expected explosion of the great glass domed roof by hiding in corners or crouching down behind the stands and displays of computers which Computex had brought together. The original thousand or so exhibitors and visitors had since been joined by about another five hundred shepherded in off the streets by the police force outside and they had spilled back into the hall to find comfort and space. All the first-aid equipment that was available had been used up on the casualties of the blizzard of glass and by the time Tel and the girl arrived not one thread of gauze or smear of ointment was left. There was, however, some food which the caterers had been attempting to ration. After only a day and a half it was clear that it would not last much longer. That evening each had a roll and a beaker of diluted orange juice. Beneath a string of rigged-up bare bulbs that looped and stretched round the hall to some distant, vaguely humming generator, the couple sat on an exhibitor's platform where Dennis, the T-shirted young man, had brought them. Tel lounged on the coconut matting floor, constantly changing position as the fibres dug into his elbow, hips and knees. Beside him, the girl rested in a wooden-armed, orange-cushioned easy chair, slowly chewing her roll. Like some of the others, her gums were bleeding. More of her hair had fallen out and small red blood spots, Tel noticed, had begun to appear under the skin on the backs of her hands. Surrounded by computers and electronic gadgetry, they seemed further than ever from the primitive, agrarian life he had begun to dream about just a few hours ago. They had been born into the twentieth century and there they were stuck. Not even an atomic bomb could blow them back to the Stone Age.

On Tel's left, one of Dennis's new friends, a young man called Steve, finished his drink with an exaggerated smack of the lips, then looked about him for something to do. His eyes landed on a man whose identity – Pritchard, Megalink UK Ltd – was still pinned to his blue-striped shirt. For a moment Tel saw the man lying among seried corpses, similar badges pinned to each, waiting for relatives or friends to come and collect.

'What do these machines do, then?'

Pritchard smiled, glad of the opportunity. He patted the white metal box at his side. 'They're personnel-function oriented. Basically the computer here is a policy and law data bank, a central system which takes any number of VDUs. Line managers can use it for points of reference as well as service. Say, for instance, you want to sack someone. You just print out the key word, "Reduncancy", and it will display on the screen company policy, union agreements, legal requirements and, given information input on the individual person concerned – you can actually link this whole system to your wages computer – it will tell you how much money such a decision is going to cost you. There's so much policy and legislation these days, it's important that managers don't go wrong. An error like that could cost the company thousands. So instead of sending your manager off on expensive training courses, you can just have one of these installed. Saves money in the long run.' He paused for a moment, looking round to see if everything was clear so far. Since there were no questions, he went on: 'Same goes for hiring somebody. If you get, say, a hundred job applicants, you can use the print-out facility to reply to each one, individually, in person. Again, this takes account of company policy and current legislation ...'

'T'riffic. Why didn't they drop the bomb when the Ideal Home Exhibition was on.'

The man looked crestfallen. 'Well, you did ask.'

'Knock it off, Steve.' The girl who spoke was sitting propped against a display board which announced: 'We'll all get on fine with Megaline'. Beside her another girl was vomiting into a plastic dustbin bag.

Since they had arrived, Tel had felt apathetic. The bursts of energy which had come through at each stage of the journey from St James's Park had petered out. Herded into this cul-de-sac, he could not bring himself even to speak with Dennis's friends beyond a yes or a no, nor did he care what they said to each other. Dennis, on the other hand, apparently had some energy left and half an hour ago had wandered restlessly off to 'have a look around'. While Tel idly watched for him, wondering if he would bring back any news worth repeating, he had noticed a woman of about forty with short hair and a dull green wool suit moving from stand to stand.

The cheer-leader, he thought, as she now began to approach them, come to hand out crumbs of comfort. She stepped up on to the Megaline platform.

'Hello.' She seemed internally sprung, bouncing at the knees and round the head and shoulders. 'How are you getting on?'

'Famous,' said Steve.

'Not so bad in here, is it?' The question was rhetorical to say the least, and the young man made a hissing sound through his teeth. 'It seems funny to think that you've only got to go twenty miles west of here and you'll find everyone is fit as a fiddle. Fresh air, nothing damaged, everything working. It's only round here that everything's in such a state.'

'Why don't you go there then?'

'I intend to.' She paused to let attention focus on her. 'In twenty minutes several hundred of us will leave through that door over there.' She nodded to the other side of the hall. 'Anybody who wants to come with us is welcome.'

Steve frowned. This was a serious proposition. 'What about the guns? They say they'll shoot anyone who tries to step outside.'

'There are three armed men at that door. Don't forget they are in the same position as we are. And we have a plan. If that fails, our numbers alone would overwhelm them.'

'I wouldn't like to bet on it.'

'It's true that they want us dead. They've got enough people to worry about as it is. It's more convenient if they keep us all here and let us die slowly and painfully from the radiation. My own feeling is that we should be the judge of whether we can live in the country. Of course it's a risk, but if we stay here we are risking nothing, we are on a certainty. We won't come out alive.'

'Won't there be policemen all over the place, not just outside here?'

'On the main roads, yes. But there are many ways out of London. Anyway, I leave it to you. In the next half an hour, people wanting to come will be joining the already extended queues by the two lavatories near the exit. You'll be told there what to do.'

She bounced off and left them in silence. There was little to discuss. Every one of them had felt, at some point, that they had been locked in here to be forgotten. It had already been more than thirty hours and no help had come. Now that somebody had actually put their worst fears into words, agreement swiftly followed. Even those not prepared for any violent confrontation could see there was safety in numbers. Some, however, like the girl, were too ill to contemplate the move. Others, like Tel, felt responsible for the sick person they were with, though Tel found it hard to know if, by himself, he would have followed Steve and the computer salesman and the others who were now gathering their meagre belongings together. He had done his share of running recently and he was very tired. Though he was sure the girl wouldn't want to go, either, he asked her anyway. Her eyes were hollow and dull and she opened her mouth to speak, changed her mind and shook her head. Tel sat back and watched the escapers leave and as the last of them departed, he was surprised to see Dennis turn up again.

'I see the Great Escape's started,' he said cheerily.

'Aren't you joining them?'

'No. I've seen what those bastards can do. Besides, I've found us a five-star hotel for the night.'

'What?'

'Just round the corner. Dead safe.' He looked at the girl. 'You'll love it. I guarantee you won't have spent a night like it in your life.'

She swallowed. 'I don't want to go anywhere.' Each word seemed to cause her throat pain.

'But you must see it. Come on, we'll carry you there.'

The reason Tel was here was because of the girl. Escaping with her had been his first aim but now, as she grew sicker, he knew that all he could hope for was to make her comfortable. 'Let's give it a try.' He lifted her gently out of the chair and carried her like a child, her arms wrapped round his shoulders, her eyes closed against the sight of other sufferers they passed as they walked down the aisle along by a wall. Turning round a screen they came to a door which Dennis held open for them. Inside, the corridor was pitch black and Tel waited for Dennis to get ahead of them to show them the way. He had better be right. He wasn't disturbing the girl for nothing. After a while Dennis's footsteps stopped and Tel pulled up, too. In the silence there was only the girl's heavy breathing. Then a metal bar was pushed back, a door swung open and the shadows of the night were let in. Stepping out, they found themselves in a yard whose far high walls they could just make out. Dennis went ahead and they followed the building to the left, reached a corner and turned right. Each step of Tel's outsized brogues seemed to say: 'Over here, over here.' On balance he would prefer not to be shot. A handle clicked and Tel stopped. Then a door squeaked open and Dennis announced: 'This is it.'

Even when they had stepped inside and Dennis had produced and lit an unexpectedly large candle sculpted in the shape of Big Ben, Tel was still none the wiser; following its brown glow, he could see nothing resembling a hotel, although his feet were silenced by a brightly patterned rug. 'Carpet Department,' Dennis whispered loudly. Then they were on unmoving escalators, walking up to the first floor. A long way away, on the landing opposite, a chink of light described the shape of a door. Otherwise there was no sign of the width or breadth of the huge windowless building.

'What on earth is this place?' Tel asked.

'Only Europe's largest furniture store. Or so it says.'

'Where is everyone?'

'Don't ask me. I've been all over it. A couple of offices seem to be occupied but I didn't knock to find out. There's no one else about. Perhaps the management locked the doors when the sirens went off. The police up the road probably helped, too, by diverting everyone on the streets into the exhibition halls.'

They had reached the second floor now and Dennis led them off through unrestrained three-piece suites, past drinks trolleys and great china tigers. Finally Dennis stopped and they saw themselves reflected in a great round mirror with two smaller ones either side set in purple suede at the back of a great lambskin-covered round bed.

'Jesus,' Tel said and he set the girl down on the edge of it. Even she had a smile.

'TV, radio, fridge,' Dennis pointed out the highlights of

the built-in extras. 'The bed's supposed to revolve, too, it says here, but I can't make it work. It must be mains electric.'

'It's great.'

'A snip, too, at £4359. Anyway, I'm going to check out a coffee lounge on the next floor down, so I'll leave you two lucky people in peace.'

He produced another large candle, this one in the shape of an alabaster column, and took a light from Big Ben which he placed beneath the large mirror at the back of the bed. Then he was off, his shadow flickering over the furniture behind him.

With effort, the girl pulled herself on to the bed and curled up. Tel lay down beside her and looked at her tarnished face, browner perhaps because of the light which filtered through the sides of the candle.

'Give me a cuddle,' she said.

She lifted her head for him to put one arm behind it. The other gripped her round the back and he pulled close against her, nuzzling to the head that was now nearly all bare. She shivered. From beyond the walls of the building came a crackling sound, indistinct at first. But as it continued and was added to, there was no mistaking the determined noise of machine-gun fire.

'It's so boring,' she said, 'having to die.'

'It's not your fault about your brother. He'll probably be all right if he was out in the open. At least there weren't any buildings to fall on him.'

'I don't know. I should have been with him anyway.'

'On the other hand a quick flash and a bang and that might have been it. Nobody really knows about these nuclear weapons. They aren't the kind of things you can try out. It's strange there hasn't been anything more. Nothing else going off, no planes flying overhead. It's quiet as a grave. I hope to God we haven't surrendered already.'

Bob grunted. Bishop was not the most sensitive of human beings. One could choose one's friends, he reflected, but one did not always have too much control over whom one would be pinned to the floor of a collapsed house with. Conversation was spasmodic, their mouths full of dust, but it was a mutual lifeline in the dark where they could not see each other even though they were little more than a yard apart. Bob's knees, crushed by the timber, no longer hurt: there was no feeling in his legs at all. But there was in his right arm, trapped beneath brick and rubble, and the pain jabbed its furious fingers down into his body. Until night had come he had managed to use his left hand to play with the pack of cards he had fished from his trouser pocket. Bishop, face down with the weight of the beam crippling his back, had had one arm clear to turn the cards over. Bad light had stopped play when Bob was just over three million pounds down. All this time the girl had been nearby, out of sight, completely buried by the rubble that came down, and they had long since given her up for dead. Bishop had mentioned how much she reminded him of his own daughter; Bob had talked about Tel.

It was hard to know about the tiredness. Every now and then Bob felt himself drifting off, images crowding in on him, of his home, of his family, of good times on the town, even of long-ago school days. Not knowing if it was sleep or unconsciousness that threatened, he struggled against it, frightened that he might not wake up again.

'How about another yell for help?' he suggested.

'My ribs wouldn't stand it. You have a go.'

With a deep breath Bob put all his energy into it but the cry he produced, an outraged call, suddenly swept up into a high note, a scream of pain brought on by the searing agony of his right arm. The note disappeared upwards, spiralling into inaudibility, into silence. He squeezed his wet eyes shut and moaned softly for a while until the worst of it had worn off.

'Bloody hellfire.'

'What was it, the arm?'

'Too right. Christ, if I had an axe I'd chop it off, no question. How's your body?'

'Ribs hurt. Can't feel anything below my waist.'

'Fun, isn't it?' Then he was silent again, gathering energy to fight his wounds. Ten minutes later he thought he might as well ask: 'What's all that between you and Alan then?'

'Oh, he's just a prick.'

'He saw you, you know, this afternoon. I was with them

when we passed by the end of the street.'

'What did he say?'

'Nothing. He carried on walking.'

'Prick. Was Beat with him?'

'Yes. I don't think she saw you, though. What is it between the three of you?'

Bishop thought for a moment before answering. The sentences came out one at a time, with pauses between each. 'Personality clash? I don't like people like him, jumped up. Looks down on you because you like steak and chips. We were all on commissions there, not just the reps but anyone who brought business in. Reed had had a client for years who he'd collected quite a tidy sum off but he screwed them up... oh, I won't bore you with details, but I happened to know someone there and they wanted to shift the business over to me. Then, about a week later, he caught his old lady with a friend of mine. There was a big row and they broke up. There was that and, well, I'm known to be a bit of a ladies' man. It must have grated. So the silly prick then tried to get me pushed out of the company. He spent days getting a dossier together, thinking I didn't know anything about it. It was rubbish, a complete waste of time.'

'How did Beat fit in?'

'Oh, she fitted in fine.' The chuckle was no more than a grumble in his aching chest. 'On the floor of her office at about five past two yesterday afternoon. Reed broke in on us. He was quite put out.'

'Well, well, well. You insurance chaps do have a busy life.'

Bob didn't want to know any more. With life so short it was small comfort to hear of a triangle that was so eternal. He began to dream.

16: GOING HOME

On the advice of Ted Evans, Maggie Blackett was going home to her tidy Georgian house which she hoped was still standing, unspoilt, eight miles away in Sedgefield. Not only had the army agreed that she could make the journey but they had also offered to provide an escort to take her back down the road nearly to Bishop Auckland, then east and over the motorway to the quiet rural town. All through the night she had known that the students, sick as they were, had been happily climbing aboard the great lorries to roll north to the observatory and the playing fields. The place she and two students had selected to 'plant' the warhead had been a good choice. It had been possible for the bulldozers to clear a path to it, there was ample room for lorries to be parked once they reached it, and it provided a distribution point for food, water, blankets, drugs and rescue equipment for a large part of the desolated area. In return, Spennymoor was receiving more of the injured, and those too badly cut and burned to be taken on to Bishop Auckland were still being cared for on the Bessemer Estate where they would find small comforts in their last days or hours.

The roaming army was a source of concern to Maggie, not for what it was doing so much as for what it might do. As far as the military junta in York was concerned, she had told Ted Evans, the district council's function was now only to take care of the barely living, the dying and the dead, to stop anyone complaining and to prevent them going anywhere that might offer some kind of safety or support. There was nothing in the Home Office circulars, she pointed out, that said otherwise. Locking up a radio enthusiast and smashing his equipment was in no statute book she knew of and she was nervous about other laws that might be waiting in ambush. When the chief executive ran across her in the car park and accused her of inventing the story of the warhead's discovery, she hotly denied it, suspecting that among the new laws one might be found to lock her away. Although they both knew

Ted was not about to run to the army with his suspicions, he told her flatly that he did not believe her. It was only a miracle, he said angrily, that half the town hadn't tried to evacuate and if that had happened he had no doubt that the Territorials, who were as nervous as anybody else, would have mown a few dozen down. But she stuck to her own guns and when he suggested she went home it was as if he were telling her she was relieved of her duties. She didn't mind. If even one poor soul in Durham was comforted by water and painkillers, then it had been worth all the rows.

Before she left, however, she went down to see Dr MacGilvray at the health centre. Like herself, he could not have slept for more than forty-four hours. Unlike her, however, he had no home to escape to. Any offers he might have had from the town meant that he would be nearby, on-call, and the chances of his being allowed to sleep undisturbed were slim. New crises, new complications, new patients diverted him at every moment and the cry of 'doctor' was never far away. The councillor's idea, therefore, was to take him with her to Sedgefield where in fifteen minutes he would find himself unmolested and unknown.

'I don't know,' he said when she found him walking back from the sports centre. By the low-voltage light from the windows she could see his red eyes and his unshaven skin stretched tight across his dry cheek bones. At that moment he looked well past retiring. 'Did you hear about my young locum?'

'What about him?'

'He joined up. One of the patients who's just arrived tells me he's seen him in Durham looking after the injured. And I thought he was getting his head down.'

'Our loss, their gain.'

'True. I think, maybe, he's happier there. There's something he's long been waiting to get off his chest.'

'But you can't let that stop you getting yourself some sleep, doctor. You'll be doing nobody any good soon.'

'I'm not already. My hands are nearly seized solid. Give me an hour to sort things out.'

'I'm not sure I can stay awake that long.'

'You had better, if you're driving. Here, have one of these.'

Awkwardly, his arthritic fingers took a small brown capsule out of his apron pocket.

'So that's how you do it. I hope it works – I'm driving your car. I'll see you outside the health centre at five.'

To pass the time Maggie went down to the police station. As far as she knew nobody had been to see Councillor Greenhalgh since Ted Evans's unsuccessful attempt to secure his release two days ago. When she arrived the detective came out to see her, smiling as if he knew her well and saying that Greenhalgh had quietened down a bit now. He might have been referring to a wayward child. The prisoner wasn't asleep, despite the hour, and he was brought into the interview room where tea was conjured up.

'First cup I've had since coming on last night,' the detective said, sitting down. He wasn't going to go away.

Councillor Greenhalgh looked at him sullenly for a moment, then sat down on the opposite side of the table and asked for the news. His appetite for it, which had brought him here in the first place, had not gone away. Between them, the detective and Maggie Blackett brought him up to date, telling him about the town, about the saintly people of the Bessemer Estate, about the army unit that went into Durham and the convoys that followed. From beyond the town was the news of the continuing fires, the congestion, like fishbones stuck in so many throats, the dozens and dozens who had been lost at sea. There was a complete block on any more people leaving Tyne and Wear, whatever their condition and in spite of the radiation that was eating into them. They were to stay where they were, take shelter and sit it out. In Newcastle the authorities were requisitioning all abandoned property, taking from it anything they deemed useful. At the border the Scots, with enough problems of organising help for Aberdeen to last them a lifetime, had prevented those fleeing from crossing into their land. To help them, peace-keeping troops had been flown in from Northern Ireland. In the south, Essex, southern Suffolk and north Kent had been declared No-Go areas which nobody was allowed to leave. The capital was sealed off. On the Continent radiation had blown across Holland and Belgium and as a precaution the populations of the Rhineland had been ordered to stay indoors for the next forty-eight hours.

'There must be a lot of people in this country a lot angrier than me,' Councillor Greenhalgh said as the reports came to an end. 'What about the Polaris submarine and the American cruiser that was damaged?'

'That seems to have blown over,' the detective said. 'It hardly gets a mention on the national news now. The army boys here say they think that what happened is that the missiles were launched through some electronic or human error. The Russian submarine that was tailing the patrol realised the warheads had taken off and thought the button had finally been pressed. So when it suddenly found an American anti-submarine vessel bearing down on it, it opened up.'

'It doesn't take much, does it? I suppose we should be thankful the Russian submarine didn't have nuclear-tipped torpedoes. Is the military still on alert?'

'I expect they will be, for a few more days, just to keep an eye on things. A lot of the regular army has been flown out.'

'I must go now,' Maggie said. 'I'm returning to Sedgefield. I expect the council will try to get you released again this morning.'

Greenhalgh shrugged. Either he thought he was better off where he was or the lethargy brought on by the radiation was getting to him. She left and went back to the health centre where MacGilvray, an old man in a tweed fishing jacket, was waiting for her. They drove back to the TAVR tent and picked up their escort, a soldier on a motorbike, and left the town, past the headlights that burned on the Trading Estate, past the acres of suffering hidden within the grey council blocks, and away to the open road south.

'Did you have any news of your friends at the Dryburn?' Maggie asked as they picked up speed.

'Not a thing. I've seen hundreds of people from Durham in the past couple of days but not one has come from the hospital.'

'What about Aberdeen? Do you have people there?'

'A nephew. Last time I saw him he told me he was the city's emergency planning officer.'

'There are always the ironies, like Pity Me. Did you notice

the pub in the main street in Spennymoor, near the health centre?'

'Which one?'

'The Polaris.'

'Oh dear.'

'Will you be going back to Scotland?'

'Nobody will be going anywhere for a long while. When the last of these patients die, the first of the next lot will come in. Cancer, leukemia, all kinds of epidemics. Then all the fish left swimming in the North Sea will be up to their gills in radiation and they'll be eaten by birds who will defecate all over the country and the crops will be sick with it and the animals will eat it ... we'll see no end to it in our lifetimes.'

'If only we could be innoculated against radiation.'

'No, no, no, that would never do. That would be just another step in the arms race. A nuclear weapon is a biological weapon. It attacks the white blood cells, bone marrow, glands, intestines, reproductive organs. If one side finds the cure, the other side will get it and then they'll switch to some other deterrent - nerve agents, toxins, anthrax, bubonic plague. They'd soon find something that Geneva conventions and SALT treaties hadn't thought of yet. Protecting yourself in an arms race only moves the process on a stage further.'

Maggie said nothing, looking ahead, keeping her eyes on the tail-light of the motorcycle in the half-light of dawn. At the bridge that crossed the motorway she slowed and they looked to the north up the road that swept by the desolation of Durham and Chester-le-Street towards the pandemonium of Newcastle. The lanes were a mess of cars and lorries and in the distance plumes of smoke still came from those burning themselves out. One northbound lane had been cleared but there was no traffic on it. The doctor rubbed his eye with the heel of his hand and Maggie asked if he was all right.

'Elephants,' he said. 'A circus caravan with jugglers and clowns on penny-farthings coming down the motorway. Just tiredness giving me a treat.' He sniffed and stretched the muscles on his face. 'Have you family?' The road block where they were stopped on the way into the town pulled him round, making him think of where they were going.

'Husband, two boys.'

'What does your husband do?'
'Solicitor.'
'And the boys?'
'One at school, one hoping to go to university in September.'
The mention of it brought it home again. It wasn't just them. There was another generation yet who wasn't going anywhere. Cleared by the policemen on duty they moved off again. Though there was hardly anybody about, it was apparent that Sedgefield had had a busy day, too. At the parish church the motorbike stopped and waved them on and they turned down a side street to pull up before a house befitting a solicitor and a local councillor. The front door was open. Two boys were coming down the path, each holding one end of a stretcher on which a body was completely covered by a blanket.

17: THE FINAL STATEMENT

At ten minutes to six on Sunday morning Vaughan Williams's music faded on radios throughout the country to be replaced by a piercing, high-pitched whine. The announcer whose voice had become familiar in the past twenty-four hours came on the air: 'This is the United Kingdom Wartime Broadcasting Service. We have just heard that the President of the United States will be making a statement to the people of the United States and her allies in Nato at six o'clock, that's ten minutes from now. This will be an important message to the people of the West. Please stay by your sets. Shortly before the President makes his statement, the Secretary of State for Foreign and Commonwealth Affairs will be talking to us here in Britain. Ensure that your radios remain switched on. In the meantime you are reminded that the curfew is still in force ...'

In Hammersmith the words crackled over the portable in the cellar and Simon woke up. He raised his head from the cushion and looked around him. No candles burned; only the radio dial and the luminous clock were visible.

'Mummy!'

Beside him John immediately came to, catching his breath as he spun in a vertigo down through which his heart thumped. But he could think of no better sound than the boy's voice to bring him out of his much-needed sleep.

'Hello, son. What's up?'

'Where's Mummy?'

'She's here. I'm here, too.'

'I want Mummy.'

'Come on, then.' He lifted the boy over him and laid him down next to Shirley. There was the small smacking noise of a thumb being sucked as she cuddled him to her, and John lay awake, waiting for the broadcast to begin. The news that had come on the air during the night had told him most of what he wanted to know. There were few surprises. Something like this had, he had been convinced, been bound to happen one day. He could be thankful that he and his family had lived through it and he could reason that if this was the nuclear disaster people like him had expected for most of their lives, it could have been worse. It could have been World War Three. Whatever hardships they might now have to face, at least Armageddon might no longer threaten. With the winds continuing to blow from the west and with the half-life of radiation hourly diminishing its strength he might risk going over to Jenny's school later that day to check that she was safe.

The first sight of Shirley when he came down the stairs would not leave him: her strange grin, her white face, her nakedness. What had happened down here in the dungeon of their home? He had asked about the man he had seen leaving by the front door and, suppressing his anger, asked if he had hurt her. But she said he hadn't. The cellar was immaculately tidy, yet she was completely disarrayed. When he had raised his voice, insisting she told him what had been going on, Simon had woken and cried, which had not been the way he had expected his son to welcome him home. 'It's all right, John. Honestly, we're all going to be all right now.' He turned on his side and put an arm out to embrace both his wife and son. Shirley did not respond. She was thinking again, about the old man, tidied away with such finality into the black plastic rubbish bag.

A dozen miles to the west, the cellar's intruder was approaching Staines and the house of an old friend of his. Crouched behind a skip, Jack was waiting for a slowly-moving army convoy to go by, at the centre of which was a huge truck with its hardware covered by tarpaulins. The curfew had made his journey a long one, forcing him down back streets where he had sometimes become lost. The police and army had grown in numbers as the damage to the buildings had diminished and now most of the chaos was caused by the authorities clearing the roads. In an hour or so he should be in his friend's house where there would be a bed, perhaps beer, even water coming out of the taps. He kept thinking about it, needing the idea of the comforts to spur him on. Throughout the journey lethargy had continually overtaken him and twice he had stopped and sat down wondering if it was worth going on. Still, he was better off here, out on the road, than in that Hammersmith cell going barmy with that woman and child. Ever since the love-making had ended he had felt guilty, unsure whether he had taken advantage, and it was that as much as the claustrophobia which had driven him out. On the other hand he had looked after her, put her fire out and got rid of the rats as well as the old man who had come storming in. It wasn't as if he had jumped on her the moment he had walked in through the door. In a few weeks, when things had settled a bit, getting back to normal, he would have a few beers with his mate and tell him all about it. That was the best way to get things into perspective.

In the distance was the sound of an aeroplane coming into land, the third since dawn to bring supplies in. The screaming engines of the first as it slowed down on the tarmac beside Terminal 3 had woken Beat and Alan up. Tucked in a corner, washed and in new clothes, they dozed together beneath a blanket. Several times in the night Alan had got up to go to the lavatory, each time trying to look cheerful, as if he were just popping in there to freshen himself up, or to take another look at the cuts on his bandaged hands to see how well they were healing. Chronic diarrhoea or continual vomiting could have meant relegation to Terminal 2. The previous night while they were being taken care of, there had been rumour that the next day would bring transport for those who had somewhere to go and now they talked of the future, of the farm, of the difficulties they might encounter.

'I know what I wanted to ask you,' Alan said. 'How does that joke of Bob's end?'

Beat smiled tightly. In the early morning her face looked neither young nor particularly fresh and light grease glinted on it from the sweat of the night. But it was a handsome face, Alan thought, a knowing and forgiving one which could tolerate in a day more than he had tolerated all his life. But he hoped that something more than tolerance would keep her by his side.

'Well, as Bob said, this man had twenty-four hours to live and he got all his money out of the bank and took his friend for a night on the town. Pub after pub, nightclub after nightclub. Eventually the friend falls down in the gutter, completely drunk, and when the first man tries to get him up to go on to another haunt, the friend says: "It's all right for you, you don't have to get up in the morning."' Alan didn't laugh and Beat shrugged. 'It's the way that you tell it.'

Among those who did not get up that morning was the girl at Olympia. On the soft, lambskin bed Tel was aroused by a strange gargling sound in her throat and in the candlelight reflected in the vast mirror he saw the grey shadows that had fallen around her upper lip and her closed eyes. In despair he clutched her close and wanted to call out her name. But he didn't know it. All he could say was: 'Don't. Please don't.' Then the breathing and the gargling stopped and he cried. He cried for her, for his family, for everything taken from him, especially the future that should have been theirs.

After a while another light flickered beside them. Without awkwardness Dennis sat on the bed and put a hand on Tel's shoulder and told him how sorry he was.

'Come on, let's see if we can find a way out of here.'

'No.'

'You can't stay here forever.'

But Tel refused to leave the girl's side.

Under the fallen masonry of the house in Chelsea his brother was struggling to distinguish dream from reality. Had he been lying here for a few minutes or a few days? Somewhere, in the part he was sure was real, Bob had heard the sound of crumbling bricks, shifting timbers and footsteps crunching carefully, but there was no question of his calling out. His muscles would not even respond to the instruction to open his mouth. But the real horror had been to open his eyes and see the lightness, the yellow glimmer of the day. That was all he saw, just the shade, splashed by ripples of green each time he blinked. He had gone blind. By way of consolation the pain in his arm had stopped and now he was hardly aware of his body at all. His mind swam in a reverie of confused images, of rats, of manhole covers, of oriental carpets and buildings falling down. Seemingly hours later he felt a slight tug at the waist of his trousers and something touched the exposed flesh of his stomach. Then he heard a crackling noise, the sound of pieces of paper being hastily flicked over. The bastards, he thought, they're taking my money. I didn't come all this way just to be looted.

Two hundred and fifty miles to the north, Maggie Blackett's reunion with her family was an emotional one. For an agonisingly short time she had imagined the body the two boys had been carrying from the house was that of her husband. But it had been a victim from the motorway, one of many brought into Sedgefield in the same way they had been housed in Spennymoor. Dr MacGilvray was offered a bed in one of the boys' rooms and Maggie showed him up to it, insisting on putting on clean sheets. One of the boys called up to say that the President of the United States was about to make his promised broadcast on the radio. She finished making the bed, then she turned to Dr MacGilvray and said: 'It might be important.'

'I'm away to bed. Not even the American President can keep me from my sleep.'

'Good night then, doctor.'

'Good night.'

She closed the door and went down the familiar stairs, happy to be back in her own home. In the kitchen her husband and the two boys were gathered round the radio set on the table where she gratefully drank down a glass of fresh orange juice. She had missed the Foreign Secretary's speech. The President had just come on the air.

'*... Modern warfare is highly complex. It relies on a backup of highly sensitive, interrelated electronic and technological systems. The missiles that were activated from the British*

Polaris submarine Resolution *in the North Atlantic on Friday last were resultant from a tape error at the North American Air Defence station which was unrectified in communications terms with the vessel in due time. However, Nato has long recognised the level of the error factor and there have always been a number of counter-measure options available to us to invalidate such an error. In the situation that developed Friday, Soviet action negated all such countermeasure options. A Soviet satellite in geostationary orbit employing laser technology interrupted the projected flight-path of the targeted missiles when they attained three degrees west of longitude. The resultant effect was to divert the missiles on an erratic and non-interceptable path and scatter them on the helpless people of Britain. This was an act of callous, unwarranted aggression.*

'The effect of the ensuing atomic explosion, as well as the dreadful suffering and death that it caused to human life, was to incapacitate radio equipment in Nato aircraft based in defence of Great Britain. As a consequence, two United States Airforce combat planes were deprived of their navigational aids and regrettably strayed over Finnish territory. The Russians' response to these crippled aircraft was to send out six Sukhoi-19 tactical strike aircraft to fatally intercept them. This was an act of unprecedented aggression.

'Two hours ago Soviet tank divisions began to enter Poland and Czechoslovakia to support those divisions already massed in East Germany and along the Warsaw Pact borders. We have had no prior indication of such manoeuvres, as is required under the treaties that exist between Nato and the Warsaw Pact. We can only interpret the movements as an act of aggression.

'One hour ago hostilities commenced at Fulda Gap, the most vulnerable position along the Rhine.

'Finally, the citizens of Moscow, Leningrad and other major Soviet cities have been ordered underground. We believe this to be an extremely hostile posture.

'There has been nothing in the history of our countries that has ever matched any one of these hostile acts. Our protests and complaints to the Soviet government over every one of these issues has been met with threats and denials and the Soviets have now withdrawn their representation at the United Nations.

'There are few options left to us. Before I began speaking to

you, I set in motion a plan agreed between our government and our allies in Europe which will reduce the ovewhelming threats the Soviets have made to the entire free world. By exploding a ten-megaton nuclear device high in the atmosphere above the USSR we can effectively incapacitate Soviet communications systems, and so eliminate the possibility of further hostile response. This is not, repeat not, a declaration of war, but we believe that this way, a way which will cause minimal bystander fatalities, is the only way to prevent our undisputed enemy from continuing to exploit the tragic situation, to stop him from advancing on our lands, our cities and our homes as he has so long wanted to do and to deny him the opportunity of extinguishing the flame of peace and freedom from our lives and our hearts forever. This counter-measure, I can now tell you with no happiness, no joy or satisfaction of revenge, has been successful . . .'

Upstairs, in the soft bed, between the crisp sheets that had made him shiver as he slid down between them, Dr MacGilvray was thinking about the work that would await him when he awoke. The task appeared impossible, but once the initial panic was over, once the size of the problem had been accurately assessed and resources allocated the struggle would be easier, energies used more effectively. As he drifted into sleep Dr MacGilvray heard the same buzzing in his ears that had interrupted his fishing expedition two days earlier. This time it grew louder and louder and as he came fully awake he realised that it was the sound of the sirens. They were going off again now. All over Europe.